Shelly has never felt such pain.

"Why him?" she asked and saw the rise of Trevor's shoulders. An unreadable mask covered his face, and a veiled expression lay in his eyes. "I didn't mean. . ." In the nightmare of the situation, Shelly wondered if she really did mean to imply that this should have happened to anyone but Don.

Trevor must have understood. "I'm sure we all wonder, Shelly. But we don't have answers like that. Just say—do—whatever you want."

"I want. . .Don."

She wouldn't look at his face, but she saw his hand reach for her, and she shrank back against the couch, away from him. "You're not Don," she said.

A helpless sound escaped his throat. He stood. She glanced up and it seemed that all the lights that had illuminated her twenty-one years of life suddenly flickered, then they began to spin, turning the world into gray confusion, and thankfully, the whispered shouts faded into the distance, and everything turned to blessed blackness.

YVONNE LEHMAN, an award-winning novelist, lives in the heart of the Smoky Mountains with her husband. They are the parents of four grown children. In addition to being an inspirational romance writer, she is also the founder of the Blue Ridge Christian Writers' Conference.

Books by Yvonne Lehman

HEARTSONG PRESENTS
HP37—Drums of Shelomoh
HP82—Southern Gentleman
HP126—Mountain Man
HP201—A Whole New World

Hawaiian Heartbeat

Yvonne Lehman

Heartsong Presents

A note from the author:
I love to hear from my readers! You may write to me at
the following address: **Yvonne Lehman**
                              Author Relations
                              P.O. Box 719
                              Uhrichsville, OH 44683

ISBN 1-57748-049-X

HAWAIIAN HEARTBEAT

Cover illustration by Peter Pagano.

PRINTED IN THE U.S.A.

one

The first thing Shelly Landon sensed was a dry scratchy throat. *Perhaps that's what woke me,* she thought, or maybe it was the November chill of a night strangely light and silent. After slipping from beneath the covers she sat on the edge of the bed in flannel pajamas, coughing and hugging her arms.

Swallowing hard, trying to clear her aching throat, she pushed her heavy mass of dark hair away from her face and walked over to the window. Then she understood the eerie hue and unusual quietness. The world outside was being inundated by giant flakes of snow that had already white-washed the campus.

A sudden gust of wind rattled the window and spat icy snow against the panes. Then she remembered there had been storm warnings. Shivering, she coughed again and looked toward her roommate, who was still sleeping soundly. After taking two spoonfuls of her cough medicine and waiting for the tickling in her throat to subside, she climbed back in bed and pulled the covers close around her chin. Her last coherent thought was of Don. *Which team won the football game?* she wondered. She'd felt too sick to stay up and listen to the sportscast. He would call first thing in the morning. Finally, she rested peacefully and drifted off to sleep.

The shrill ringing of the telephone awakened her. A groan sounded from across the room, and Shelly knew Peggy was groping to answer it.

"Shelly, it's for you," Peggy said sleepily.

Shelly turned over far enough to stick her arm out from under the quilt. "Hello," she said sleepily, expecting to hear Don's voice ask how she was feeling, apologize for waking her, and tell her who won the game.

"Shelly, honey. This is your mother," the voice said, almost too low for Shelly to hear.

"Mom?" Shelly questioned with a raspy sound. Her mother knew better than to call on Saturday morning. That always had been her sleep-in day. Strange, too, that she identified herself, as if Shelly didn't know her own mother's voice.

"Shelly, honey," she said again, pausing to take a deep breath. "I have some unpleasant news."

"What is it, Mom?" Shelly almost shouted, and the force of her words brought on another coughing spell. She sat up in bed, not noticing her covers fall away or the coldness of the room. Her heart throbbed against her chest. Was it her dad? He'd always been healthy. What was wrong?

"Is Peggy there?" her mom asked.

"Yes, Mom. Peggy's here. What is it?" By this time Peggy was sitting on the edge of her bed, staring and mouthing, "What's wrong?"

Then her mother's words came quickly. "Don is in the hospital, Shelly. There was an accident. It must have been the sleet and ice that caused it. Nobody's sure yet."

"Mom," Shelly wailed, "is he all right?"

"We don't know. It was pretty bad. Your father and I are here with Margo and Hanlan. Trevor's on his way with Gran, and Don's sisters have been notified."

"I'll come, Mom," she said, tossing the covers aside and standing. "What hospital?"

"No, Shelly," her mom answered quickly, her voice distressed. "You must not come. It was the whole bus. There isn't room for anyone else. I was so frightened that you might have been involved. I'm so thankful you weren't."

"But Don's. . .going to be okay?" she stammered, feeling helpless.

"The doctors are with him," her mother answered. "There has been no time for them to talk to any of us. The coach was not badly hurt, so he is notifying relatives. I thought I'd better tell you before it came on the news." She hesitated. "Shelly, why didn't you go to the game?"

"Just a little sore throat," Shelly answered. That seemed so unimportant now. "Let me know the minute I can see him."

"I will, honey. You pray."

Pray? Yes. From the moment her mother mentioned the accident, her heart, soul, and mind had been silently praying, *God, don't let him be hurt. Not Don.*

They hung up.

Shelly told Peggy about the accident. "I should have been with him," she wailed.

"It's a miracle you weren't," Peggy replied thankfully.

"But I wish I had been. Don and I have always been insepa-rable. Almost like one person." She gestured helplessly. "But you know that."

Peggy's tousled blond curls bounced as she nodded and took the cold tablet bottle from Shelly's shaking fingers. She flipped off the lid, took out a tablet, then brought Shelly a cup of water.

Even after she turned the thermostat up and sat on the bed with the quilt wrapped around her shoulders, Shelly continued to shake. Normally, she would have been with Don. This was one of the few football games she'd ever missed.

Suddenly, everything came alive throughout the dorm. While Shelly shivered in spite of the blanket, Peggy left to find out what she could. Soon, she returned. There'd been an early news bulletin concerning the bus load of football players that apparently swerved to miss a tractor-trailer and lost con-trol on the icy highway. It went over a steep embankment. Details would not be announced until relatives had been noti-fied. The van of cheerleaders had made it back safely last night.

Shelly felt the blood drain from her face and a cold clammy feeling moved over her body. *God, don't let him be hurt. Not . . .seriously. Please.*

"Why don't you get dressed, Shelly?" Peggy suggested. "So you will be ready when they come to take you to see Don."

Grateful for the suggestion of something to do, Shelly showered, then blow-dried her black hair that hung in natural curls down her back. It seemed a stranger with dark brown eyes that appeared almost black against her pale skin stared back at her from mirror. She applied cover-stick to hide the purplish circles under her eyes and brushed her cheeks with color.

Applying makeup seemed like a foolish ritual at a time like this, but she wanted to look as good as possible for Don in hopes that he wouldn't know how scared she felt. Her wide jawline looked even wider because it was unbroken by her pale unsmiling lips. A touch of lip gloss helped a little. At least the effort gave her something to do to keep from screaming.

She stared a moment longer. Could that be her in the mirror? Always before, hers had been a happy face with dark flashing eyes, flushed cheeks, and a mouth that was never still—perhaps due to years of cheerleading in high school, then college. And she'd always been accused of being a chatterbox. This silent, brooding face was a most uncommon sight. She'd known, of course, how important Don was to her, but this. . .this just confirmed it in a different way. The thought had never entered her mind that. . .no, she would not think the worst. God would not let anything bad happen to Don. She prayed. She asked. She begged.

She tried not to listen to others talking and crying in the hallway as she reached into her closet for something presentable, then dressed in a simple pale green blouse and a long tweed skirt. She laid out a camel-colored blazer and stepped into brown scrunched-suede boots, then fastened small gold earrings and added a chain on which hung Don's class ring.

Peggy, looking pale, kept making small talk that Shelly barely heard as she went to the window where she'd stood in the middle of the night. Being three stories up, it overlooked much of the campus, including one of the larger parking lots. She started to turn back, but a long black car pulled into the parking lot—not the kind students drove. A man and woman got out and hurriedly, though carefully, headed through the snow toward the dorm. Shelly instinctively knew the couple had come to take a family member of a football player to the hospital.

Slowly, she realized that other students were feeling as she was—afraid, bewildered, hopeful, prayerful, dazed. She could name all the close friends of the players: Julie, Donna, Jill, Karen, and on and on and on.

She warned herself not to worry needlessly. Don would want her to think positive thoughts. She gazed at the whitened world. It was the kind of weather when Don would normally be out there tossing snowballs up at the window, yelling for her to come down or he'd come up and drag her down and make a snow-woman of her. They would spend the day skiing, sledding, sliding, snowball fighting, or just rolling in the snow, laughing.

Don would probably appear any minute with his golden hair sparkling with light flakes of snow, his blue eyes shining with mischief, his athletic frame eager for vigorous activity, his laughter reflecting his heart of gold. He would appear, and she would be surrounded by that wonderful glow of love and togetherness the two of them had shared for twenty-one years. A smile touched her lips as thoughts of Don warmed her heart.

Suddenly, her eyes zoomed back to the parking lot. Joy flooded her heart as she glimpsed the top of a blond head when someone emerged from a car. But Don wouldn't pull the fur collar of his jacket up to cover his ears or bend his head to shield his face from the snow and wind.

She gasped.

Peggy stood up from where she was making her bed. "Shelly, what is it?"

She turned her back to the window and faced Peggy. Terror sounded in her voice. "It's Trevor!"

"Trevor?"

"Trevor Steinbord."

"Trevor Steinbord," Peggy repeated with a lift of her chin. A light came into her eyes. "Oh! The writer."

"Don's older brother," Shelly said. "Trevor always brings bad news."

Peggy touched Shelly's arm. "Come on, Shelly," she pleaded gently.

"No, it's true," she moaned and felt a sudden flash of heat. One moment she felt clammy cold, the next it seemed that sweat was about to dribble all over her. It probably would, for the worst part of her always surfaced when Trevor was near.

"You see, Peggy, it was Trevor who took me to the hospital when Don had appendicitis and when Don broke his arm. He's the one who came when we were children and informed me that Don had the measles. Oh, and so many other things. He would not just. . .come to see me, Peggy. I know."

Peggy tried to console her. "They probably sent him because of the bad roads."

But in her heart, Shelly knew, even though her mind refused to accept it. Her turmoil was replaced by an unnatural calm. Even her sweat turned cold, like beads of ice. It was like the first time she'd walked out to the edge of the high dive when her foot was too far out for her to back up and there was no place to go but down.

She walked out into the hall and down two flights of stairs. It seemed she didn't breathe. Upon reaching the lobby, she saw Trevor talking to the resident mother. He was wearing dark blue pants and a suede jacket, the fur collar now turned down. Snowflakes had melted on his hair, turning it into damp curls, like it would have done to Don's.

He hurried to her, his face stricken and his voice a whisper. "Shelly."

"I could have driven—" she began raspily, then coughed.

Trevor led her to a couch. She leaned against its back, but he sat on the edge, facing her. The TV was on, and a few students sat around it, probably awaiting the horrible newscast.

The sound faded. Shelly had to look away from the moist grief in Trevor's eyes. "You always tell me such terrible things, Trevor," came her raspy whisper. "Please don't."

"I have to say it, Shelly," came his strangled words. "I'm so sorry. I loved him too."

Loved, he said—in the past tense. "You're lying," she moaned. "You always come with morbid tales of woe. I won't listen." She could say no more. She tried to shake her head as if that would cause Don to appear in Trevor's place, but all it did was make the world whirl. She didn't want to hear anything Trevor had to say about her beloved Don. Nor did she wish to look at him and see again his strong resemblance to his brother whom she loved so dearly.

"Why him?" she asked and saw the rise of Trevor's shoulders. An unreadable mask covered his face, and a veiled expression lay in his eyes. "I didn't mean. . ." In the nightmare of the situation, Shelly wondered if she really did mean to imply that this should have happened to anyone but Don.

Trevor must have understood. "I'm sure we all wonder, Shelly. But we don't have answers like that. Just say—do—whatever you want."

"I want. . .Don."

She wouldn't look at his face, but she saw his hand reach for her, and she shrank back against the couch, away from him. "You're not Don," she said.

A helpless sound escaped his throat. He stood. She glanced up and it seemed that all the lights that had illuminated her twenty-one years of life suddenly flickered, then they began to spin, turning the world into gray confusion, and thankfully, the whispered shouts faded into the distance, and everything turned to blessed blackness.

Awareness returned slowly. First it came in the strong odor of ammonia in her nasal passages, along with the smell of rubbing alcohol. Then there was a white blur as busy hands applied a cold wet cloth to her face. She felt a coughing spell coming on and opened her eyes. Nearby sat a figure, dressed in dark blue, topped with golden hair that looked like someone had mussed it.

"Don?" she gasped on a cough and managed to get her arm around the white blur in order to stretch her hand toward him. The figure moved, but he didn't reach for her. Instead, he leaned forward, balanced his elbows on his thighs, and covered his face with his fingers.

two

Five months later, spring had come, but it was still winter in Shelly's heart. She stood on the front deck of her home in the Blue Ridge Mountains of North Carolina, looking out over the golf course and toward the backdrop of surrounding mountains. The slight April breeze stirred her dark hair.

Her father came out and fingered a curl that lay almost to her waist, against the pine-green silk blazer she wore with beige slacks and flats. "Why the long face, Kitten?" he asked gently.

"Just thinking," she said and gave him a genuine smile. She was very aware of his love for her and knew that her withdrawal saddened both him and her mother. She was their only child, born when they were in their mid-thirties, and they had centered their world around her. Many times in the past months her father had said, "I wish we doctors had a cure for broken hearts."

But there was none. Everyone said time would heal the pain, but she could only wonder how much time it would take.

"You don't want to go tonight, do you, honey?" her father asked.

"Not really, Daddy. It doesn't mean anything now."

A look of sadness crossed his face before he could conceal it, but he forced his voice to sound light. "Well, I wasn't going to tell you, but you force my hand. Tonight at the Steinbords', your mother and I are going to tell you about your graduation present."

"Oh, Daddy," she said, turning to face him. It touched her that her family and the Steinbords tried so hard to spark some interest in her. As a doctor's daughter, she was well aware of the reality of life and death. This knowledge, however, had

13

not prepared her for Don's death.

She had never before questioned God and how He could allow such things to happen. Don had been such a good Christian. He would have done wonderful things in the world. Shelly dared not tell anyone how greatly her faith had been shaken. She was going through the motions of life, but it was not easy without Don.

"I don't mean to be such a pain, Daddy. But. . .why give me the present at the Steinbords?"

"You know that Margo Steinbord likes to make a production of things, Shelly. She wants to tell you about their present."

"What is it?" she asked, pretending to be enthused.

"Uh huh," he joked with a twinkle in his dark blue eyes. "You must come to dinner or you get no present."

"You're bribing me," she accused.

"And you're smiling," he said gently. "That's a beautiful thing to see."

She kept the smile on her lips but turned to look toward the landscape. She heard her mother open the screen door.

"Margo will refuse to serve us if we wait a minute longer," Mother warned.

"Are you taking the car?" Shelly asked.

"I wouldn't dare let your mother walk on the street looking like that." His eyes admired his wife, Nancy, from the top of her head, down the blue silk dress, to the tips of her high-heeled shoes.

"Thank you, sir," she replied, her own coy gaze taking in his handsome pin-striped suit. "For that, you get a reward." She kissed him on the cheek.

I'll never have a love like that, Shelly thought. "I think I'll walk," she said.

She watched with love and pride as her parents walked down the steps toward the Buick parked in the driveway. She viewed them differently than she had a few months ago. They were not just her parents, but a couple, private unto them-selves. They were a handsome pair—her dad tall and her mom of medium height like Shelly. Both had black hair, a product of Italian ancestry somewhere in the background of each. Her mom's had a few gray hairs mingled in, and her dad's was white at the temples. Shelly had always anticipated a marriage like theirs for herself and Don.

After the car pulled out onto the street, Shelly began walking toward the Steinbords'. They lived three houses away, but the yards were spacious and the houses far apart. Her glimpse through the rows of pines revealed golfers trying to hit their little white balls into tiny holes.

Shelly remembered walking on the golf course in two inches of snow during Christmas time. She'd recovered from her bout of flu and had passed her exams. Both seemed to have occurred without any particular effort on her part. Then, so did her walking. She had been alone, without anyone with whom to romp or play or laugh.

She'd wandered aimlessly along, almost blinded from the glare of white. Then she'd looked across the road at the Steinbords' house on the hill and saw someone standing at their living-room window. The shadowy figure might have been anyone, but she instinctively knew it was Trevor.

He always seemed to watch her at the wrong times and know the worst about her. He would know that she walked alone because of her desolation and grief. She resented his knowing. When she realized that she stood like a tree rooted beneath the frozen ground, she turned sharply and walked determinedly through the snow toward her own house, hoping Trevor would realize he had intruded upon her solitude.

"Fore," a golfer called, and Shelly's attention returned to the present and the side of the road, where yellow jonquils heralded the season.

She paused for a moment at a particular spot and remembered an incident that had not come to mind in years. She had been five years old and her furry yellow kitten died. She and Don buried it between two pines at the side of the road. They used a rock for a tombstone. Don saw Trevor washing his

father's car in their driveway and called him over to preach
the funeral service. In her childish estimation, Shelly thought
Trevor did a fine job of preaching, but even then, she didn't
quite trust his words.

Later, when she thought no one was around, she sneaked
down to the burial spot and dug up the cat. Then suddenly,
Trevor had been there, asking what was wrong.

"I knew it wouldn't work if you did it," she'd accused. "My
kitty-cat did not go to heaven. It's still here." She'd sobbed,
uncontrollably.

He'd knelt in front of her and quietly explained about the
cat's soul going to cat heaven where it would get a new body
that couldn't be sick or die.

Shelly's bottom lip had stuck way out past the upper one.
She peeked at him through her tears. "I don't believe you,"
she said, nevertheless hoping.

"Ask your mother," he'd said and stood. She had to bend
her neck back so far to look up at him that it hurt.

She ran up the street toward her own house. "I think you
tell fibs," she accused, when she felt a safe distance away.
"And you're a. . .a. . .teenager!"

That was the worst thing she could think of at the time, but
he hadn't appeared insulted. He laughed, and she felt he was
laughing at her, so, she disliked him intensely. After her
mother explained about the kitten, and the body and soul,
Shelly had disliked Trevor even more because he knew she
didn't know things. And he would think she should have her
mouth washed with soap because she'd called him a teenager.

Shelly's thoughts returned to the present when she came to
the Steinbords' driveway. Their families were the best of
friends, with much in common. They attended the same
church, Nancy and Margo volunteered at the hospital, and the
men held respected positions—Hanlan Steinbord as an archi-
tect and Shelly's father as a physician. Gran was more like a
grandmother to Shelly than her own grandparents, who lived in
other states. Shelly loved the Steinbords dearly: Hanlan and

Margo; Don, of course; and his older sisters, Betsy and Katrina. Both sisters were married, and Betsy had a baby and a toddler.

But to be honest, Shelly did not like Trevor. He had seldom been home during the past years—perhaps that's why she always felt so uncomfortable around him. Regardless, the fact remained.

Whenever Trevor was away, Shelly felt perfectly at ease with her second family. She was glad he wouldn't be at the Steinbords' dinner. He had left right after the New Year. She hadn't asked where he was going, nor when he would return.

Knowing what awaited her, Shelly smiled as she walked up the long, sweeping drive to the large contemporary house that Hanlan Steinbord had designed for his family. She wasn't disappointed as they greeted her with hugs and kisses.

Shelly joined the Steinbords as they sat around the long table near the front windows from which they could see the panoramic view, similar to the scene from the Landons' dining room. She was especially grateful to Gran, who sat across from her, sending silent signals of love with her warm blue eyes. Gran had had her bout with the flu during the winter too, and Don's death had taken its toll. The older woman's hair had turned from gray to snow-white, and she seemed more subdued than she had a few months ago. Her faith seemed stronger. . .but her body seemed more frail.

"I've told everybody else, Shelly," Katrina said during dinner. "I'm going to have a baby."

Shelly expressed delight, and Gran repeated what she'd said a thousand times. "There's nothing like babies to remind us of God's miracles and His love. I hope each of you have dozens."

Katrina and Betsy looked at each other and groaned.

"Why didn't Trevor ever marry and have children?" Shelly asked impulsively.

It was as if a conductor had cut the air with his baton and stopped the music. Everyone grew silent and looked down at his plate. An uncomfortable moment passed before Margo said quietly, "He never said."

"I'm sorry," Shelly apologized. "I didn't mean to intrude where I shouldn't."

"Shelly Landon," Hanlan boomed across at her. "You can't possibly intrude, because you're as much a part of this family as anybody else here. You say anything you want, any time you want."

Betsy piped up. "And they'll refuse to answer you any time they want."

They all laughed, and then Hanlan asked if it was time for dessert.

"Where he puts it all, I'll never know," Margo said.

"I think it's time we gave Shelly her graduation present," Philip Landon suggested.

"How do you know I'll graduate?" Shelly quipped.

"After the expense of four years at that college?" He feigned indignation. "You'll graduate!"

They all laughed.

"Well, do I have to guess?" Shelly asked, assuming a playful mood. "I'll bet it's a new car. You know how I've wanted one of those little, low, long, sleek—"

"Hey, hold on," her dad said, lifting his hand. "You're way off track."

"It's a trip, darling," her mother said. "I thought we would take a cruise around the Caribbean. See all the islands. You can relax and enjoy the summer."

"That sounds wonderful," Shelly said, but loneliness welled up, even as the others were talking excitedly about the trip. She and Don had planned on marrying following their graduation. He would have given her an engagement ring at Christmastime. They would have had a honeymoon trip this summer.

Shelly tried to feel enthused, but instead she felt guilty because everyone was trying so hard to help her through this most difficult period of her life. Both families had always been wonderful and generous. She forced herself to concentrate on what was being said.

"You know we've set up scholarships in memory of Don," Hanlan said. His voice broke. The fork in Gran's hand shook before she laid it on her plate and looked at it.

"There will be a ceremony right before the senior dance," Margo said quietly. "Trevor has volunteered to represent the family. We hope you will go, Shelly, since you were closer to Don than anyone."

They were waiting for her to respond.

"If you don't have an escort Shelly, you can go with Trevor," Margo suggested.

Shelly could only stare at the woman.

"But if you already have an escort. . ." Margo added helplessly.

Her mother's words finally registered. "Do you have an escort for the event, Shelly?"

How could they think such a thing? "I hadn't planned to go. And," she added, shaking her head in disbelief, "I would not have gone with anyone if I had been asked."

She looked at the faces surrounding her. How could she refuse their request? Any of the people sitting around that table would give her the world if I could. Don's death was their loss too, and she had witnessed some of their grief—and their bravery. The Steinbords had never asked much of her. Couldn't she make an appearance. . . for Don?

Perhaps going through the motions would serve some purpose. What was one miserable evening with Trevor? But she wouldn't really be with Trevor. In her heart and mind, she would be with Don. And as usual, with his uncanny instincts, Trevor would know that.

Smiling weakly, she said, "But given that they will be presenting the first scholarships in memory of Don, how could I refuse? I'll go to the presentation with Trevor, and we can leave the dance early."

three

"I can hear John now," Peggy wailed, stepping into her high heels. "He'll say, 'Women! Always late!' shake his head and grin like the Cheshire cat!" She bent down to look into the mirror, applied lipstick, and blotted it. "Why can't I ever make a liar out of him?"

Shelly laughed. "At least he always waits for you."

"True," Peggy admitted with a grin, then sat at the dresser to put the finishing touches to the short golden curls framing her pretty face. Her eyes, the same color green as her dress, met Shelly's in the mirror. "And I'll be waiting downstairs to make sure you go out that front door, headed for the presentation and dance with the world's most eligible bachelor."

"Oh, Peg, stop trying to brainwash me," Shelly scolded. "You know perfectly well the last place I want to be is at a dance and the last person on earth I want to be with is Trevor Steinbord."

"But you're going!" Peggy declared.

Shelly nodded, choking back the uneasiness she felt rise to her throat.

Peggy, ignoring the fact that John was waiting, took Shelly's dress out of its protective bag and lay it across Shelly's bed.

"Thanks," Shelly intoned quietly.

They both knew the thanks was for Peggy's friendship and caring during the past difficult months.

Then with a pert lift of her chin and excitement glowing in her eyes, Peggy left the room.

Shelly marveled that she had once been as exuberant as Peggy about life. She didn't expect to ever feel that way again. But she was determined not to present a morbid face to the world for the rest of her life.

20

She enhanced the natural beauty of her face by applying a moisturizer. Spring sunshine had already tanned her skin and blushed her cheeks. A hint of turquoise made her brown eyes appear even larger. She grimaced against the thought that her dewy, rose-colored lips had not been kissed in six months—would never be kissed.

With a quick movement, she loosened her hair from the restricting headband and brushed her long curls.

She stood and slipped into the dress that Margo Steinbord had made for the occasion. Viewing her image in the mirror, she admitted that Margo had exquisite taste. The deep-pink satin dress looked marvelous, as if it came directly from a designer in Paris. Her fingers touched the satin ruffle that draped over her left shoulder, crossed down the front of the bodice, and ended at the waist on the right side.

Don would have loved it, she thought, and pain stabbed her heart. Trying to ignore it, she adjusted her ruby drop-earrings and pasted on a fake smile.

She picked up Trevor's purple orchid, which had been delivered that afternoon, and fastened it at her waist, where the ruffle ended. Don had always given her roses.

The phone rang. The dorm mother said Trevor was in the lobby. Shelly felt her stomach turn over and her palms grow moist. She mentally reprimanded herself for allowing Trevor to affect her that way. She quickly slipped into her high-heeled evening shoes. A final glance in the mirror made her grateful that eight years of cheerleading had kept the fat away. She took a deep breath, walked out, and closed the door behind her.

In the privacy of the narrow stairwell, Shelly lectured herself about remaining cool. After all, Trevor couldn't force her to stay with him if the evening became unbearable.

She entered the lobby, grateful for the glare of light, the blare of a TV, and the animated greetings of well-meaning college students who, six months ago, had watched her overnight turn from extrovert to recluse.

A couple of comments were whispered in her ear to the effect that Trevor Steinbord was the most handsome, most famous man they'd ever seen and suggested that she was the luckiest girl in the world. She didn't look at Trevor directly, but she could tell that he towered over everybody and was attracting attention, particularly from the women. By now, Don would have rushed to her, put his arm around her, and told her she was gorgeous. He would have made her feel incredibly loved, secure, and wonderfully happy.

But Trevor did not approach her. He just stood—waiting. Then her friends drifted away. She had no choice but to look at him, walk toward him. A flash of hot white heat spread over her and she felt as if her skin would burst into flame. She must surely look as flushed as the rose color of her dress. Acutely aware of every sound, she heard the click of her heels against the marble floor and the swish of the satin with each step she took.

She felt like turning and racing back up the stairs. But, their primary purpose tonight was to bring honor to Don's name. That thought brought some perspective. She concentrated on the fact that Trevor's physical likeness to Don accentuated their differences.

Don had been the object of her affection as far back as she could remember, while Trevor had been a constant source of irritation. She had loved to look into the eyes that reflected the clear blue of a summer sky, but avoided the one whose eyes held the blue-gray sheen of burnished steel. One had evoked confidence in her; the other an unidentifiable uneasiness. She'd always kidded Don about resembling a blond Viking, and his blue eyes would twinkle. Trevor's eyes were guarded, and his lips remained silent. He was taller than Don, but not as muscular, for Don had had eight years of high school and college football. She had no idea what Trevor did to stay so toned.

Don had looked like he'd never met a stranger, yet he'd made it obvious that Shelly was the most important person in the world to him. Trevor's facial lines were leaner, causing his cheekbones to appear higher. That gave him an aloof appearance, which Shelly felt was also a part of his personality.

She did not tell Trevor that he looked dignified in the oyster-white tux with white velvet lapels, white pleated shirt, and bow tie. Probably every girl who had come through the lobby had made that clear to him. His eyes did not twinkle like Don's, but held a gray, distant expression as if something inside him were being suppressed.

"Shelly," he said simply.

"Trevor," she intoned. Then, determined to be as civil as possible, she asked politely, "Enjoy your afternoon?"

"The faculty and administration went to great lengths to make me feel welcomed and comfortable," he replied just as formally and opened the door for her to exit.

As they walked out to the car, Shelly took a deep breath to force herself to relax and keep herself from running back to her dorm room. Trevor held the car door open for her to slide into the passenger side of his father's Lincoln, which he usually drove when in the area.

When he got into the driver's seat, the glinting rays of the fast-retreating sun struck his hair, turning his carefully groomed waves to gold. Memories struck deep into Shelly's heart. Then her eyes met his, and she knew he realized she thought of Don.

"Why are we doing this?" she asked helplessly.

"Because it's necessary," he replied bluntly and started the engine. "I believe it's called crawling."

She shook her head. "I don't know how you could be a writer. "You speak in riddles."

He steered the car out into the street. A grin played at the corners of his mouth. "The critics think I'm intelligent if they can't understand me." He turned his face toward her and asked, "You won't tell, will you?"

Shelly's puzzlement was obvious. How could one follow or

even contribute to such a nonsensical conversation?

"There was a time years ago," he added, driving along the tree-lined street, "that you asked me not to tell."

Then she remembered! It was one of her early embarrassing experiences involving Trevor. It had occurred at Don's sixth birthday party. "I was a child," she said defensively. "Only six years old."

"Yes," Trevor replied, "but the rivalry between Don and all the other little boys was already apparent. Don hadn't learned to share you, and he fought over you several times a day."

"That started in the first grade," she said, feeling a smile coming on with the memory. "I didn't want him to fight at his own birthday party. I felt it would be my fault. So I let the other boys gorge me with equal amounts of cake and punch." She laughed softly, remembering. "But each time, I had to take one more bite from Don or one more sip of punch."

"Finally, when you could take no more," Trevor added, "you ran to an upstairs bathroom and threw up."

"That's when you came in." She turned in the seat to watch his face. "You gave me a washcloth and told me to wash my face."

"And I also told you," Trevor teased, glancing over, "that you were too pretty to let the boys make you eat all that cake and you'd get fat."

"Oh, how I hated you for seeing me like that," she groaned.

"Yes," Trevor said distantly, watching the road. "I know." He maneuvered the car around a corner and searched for a parking space near the Conference Hall where the evening's events were being held. Shelly suddenly realized that she had never been on a date with anyone but Don.

"Now listen," Trevor said, intruding upon her thoughts. "If you persist in letting your face reflect a depressed state of mind, I'll be forced to tell how you threw up all over the bathroom, leaving me to clean it up."

"I cleaned it up," she protested.

"Ha!" he exclaimed. "What does a six-year-old kid know

about cleaning up after herself? There was carpet on that bathroom floor. As soon as you left, I went to work!"

"You? You really cleaned it up?"

He nodded. "And I was fourteen. That was quite demeaning for a teenager who thought he was a man. That's why I never told. Didn't want anyone to know what lengths I'd go for a saucy little six-year-old girl with black curls and a bow in her hair."

He maneuvered the car into the parking space and switched off the engine. Something disconcerting gleamed in his eyes. He spoke softly, as if serious. "You were wearing pink that day, too. The bow. The dress. Little pink socks. And to match were little pink—"

"Oh, Trevor," she objected, put off not so much by the foolishness of his talk but by the foolishness of their sitting in the car, as if they were friends or something. "You're sick. Absolutely sick," she flung at him, as he laughed heartily. To hide her smile, she got out of the Lincoln and slammed the door shut.

She'd never heard him joke like that—not with her, any-way. They'd never had anything in common but unpleasant childhood memories of each other. His lips still smiled when he came around the car to walk beside her up the steps, but now his fathomless eyes reverted to some mysterious realm.

Entering the Conference Hall was like entering another world—a world of dim lights, crazy shadows, laughter, talking, and soft music. Blue-jeaned girls had become elegant ladies in long gowns, and rough-housing boys were transformed into handsome gentlemen in tuxes with tails.

Shelly and Trevor stood, looking around for a moment, when Peggy and John came up behind them. "We're all seated at the same table for the dinner," Peggy said. "Want to join us now or would you rather mix with some of the crowd?"

Trevor glanced at his watch. "It's almost time for the schol-arship presentations. Let's go ahead and get settled at our places." Trevor seated Shelly. Almost immediately, the college president asked for everyone's attention, and the ceremony began.

"I didn't know you would be giving a speech!" Shelly hissed under the noise of the applause when Trevor was introduced.

He winked and said, "You didn't ask." Then he strode to the podium before she had a chance to reply.

Shelly was stunned by Trevor's speech. He spoke of how not only Don, but all the deceased young men had made an impact upon those around them. Then he stressed the importance of the quality of each life rather than the number of years it lasted. She had to admit his words were eloquent and fitting. The sound of sniffles and the silent sheen of tears filled the hall.

Shelly stood with the other students as they applauded at the end of Trevor's speech, but she held her hands at her side and refused to shed the tears that threatened to spill over. She was afraid that once she began crying, she'd never be able to stop. She was glad Don was in heaven with God, but that did not alleviate her personal sense of loss. If only she didn't have to sit through the dinner and at least a little of the dance that would follow. There was no gracious way to avoid the next couple hours, however, and she was determined to endure this for the Steinbords, and for Don.

Once the ceremony was over and waiters began serving dinner, Trevor gave Shelly a knowing look and immediately began asking Peggy and John about themselves. Grateful for the cover, Shelly managed to eat some of the food and smile at the right moments in the conversation.

They were just beginning the dessert course when Peggy mumbled, "Uh, oh. What did we do? Looks like Dr. Enos is headed straight for us."

The president of the college spoke to them and held out his hand toward Trevor, who stood. "I didn't have the opportunity to speak to you after the service, Trevor, but I wanted you to know how much we appreciate your taking part. I'm sure everyone, including the students, was greatly moved by your words."

While Trevor thanked him, Dr. Enos looked at the others sitting around the table as if expecting confirmation. Each of them smiled and nodded.

"I've read a couple of your novels and am looking forward to the others," Dr. Enos complimented, returning his attention to Trevor. "Thanks again, and enjoy yourselves."

"Thank you, sir," Trevor replied to the older man, returning his friendly smile. He took his seat again as the president walked away.

"I didn't know you were a writer," John said.

"You're probably the only person on campus who didn't," Peggy said. "Haven't you heard of *Trevor Steinbord,* the best-selling author?"

"Sure, who hasn't?" John said, "But you're not. . ." His voice broke off and he blushed. "I can't believe I didn't put it together."

Shelly's attention drifted off as her three companions launched into a discussion of Trevor's work. Her gaze fell on the couples who had started dancing. *I'll never be held in a man's arms like that again,* she thought. As an all-too-familiar ache filled her heart, she wrenched her eyes away. She mustn't let herself think such thoughts or she'd end up making a fool of herself and ruining a perfectly good evening for the rest of her classmates.

As soon as there appeared to be a break in the flow of conversation at the table, Shelly looked over at Trevor. "Could we go?" she asked.

Trevor stood and extended his hand to John and Peggy, saying he was glad to have met them. With a trace of chagrin, she surmised he was as eager as she for the evening to end.

Offering his arm, Trevor said softly, "Shall we?" His other hand rested lightly on hers as he guided her across the dance floor to the exit.

As the orchestra's soft music filled her mind, Shelly felt so engulfed by a deep longing to be held in Don's strong arms that she rested her head against Trevor's jacket. She felt his arm tighten and his chin graze the top of her head.

For an instant—only an instant—she pretended he was Don.

For an instant—only an instant—Trevor pretended Shelly cared for him.

four

Embarrassed by her display of weakness, Shelly whispered, "I need some air," and raced toward the nearest door.

Outside, when she headed for the parking lot, Trevor asked, "Could we walk for awhile?"

Rather than make a scene, Shelly walked beside him to the lake. The music faded and the sounds of the night were gentle. Beneath a silvery moon, the cool breeze whispered in the treetops. Night birds called to their mates, insects sang, and water trembled over a dam. A duck's wings fanned the air as it left the water, then it waddled along the bank.

Uneasy, Shelly mumbled, "Did you have fun tonight?" She did not know how to make conversation with Trevor.

He stood looking out over the lake toward the distant trees. After a long moment, he turned toward Shelly. "I didn't come here tonight to have fun, Shelly. I came here for you. I knew you'd want to be there when Don was remembered, but I didn't want you to face that pain alone."

So this was all his idea! Shelly jerked back and swatted at something flying toward her head.

"Just a moth, looking for the light," Trevor said. "Be still." He smoothed her hair and replaced the errant strands behind her shoulder. "Gone," he said. "He must have been drawn to your perfume. What's the fragrance?"

"Beautiful."

He smiled down at her. "I might have known."

Shelly looked away, uncertain what he meant by that, then remembered that it was Katrina who had introduced her to "Beautiful" at Christmas time. He probably realized this was the same fragrance that his sister sometimes wore.

"My feet aren't accustomed to wearing such high heels on

concrete," she complained, making a face.

She thought they might return to the car. However, he gestured toward a bench several yards away. "Let's sit over there until your feet are rested," he suggested. "It's not as light there, so the insects won't bother you.

When they reached the bench, he wiped the seat with his handkerchief. Shelly sat, then stretched her feet out in front of her and wiggled them to keep the circulation going, and then decided, on impulse, to remove her shoes.

"Shelly," he began, getting right to the point. "What are your plans for the future?"

"My future?" An ironic laughed escaped her throat. She saw nothing in her future.

"Yes," he said. "Are you planning to fall in love someday, get married, have children? Are you planning a career? You graduate in two weeks. What are your plans, Shelly?"

Her gaze fell to the pink satin gown, and she ran her index finger in a pattern over the smooth material. Trevor had a way of bringing things to the surface. He could not let things be. She should have insisted on returning to the dorm the moment they left the dance.

"Sometimes, Trevor," she murmured, "I think you were placed on this earth to either haunt or taunt me."

He laughed lightly. "Now you're getting close to reality."

Shelly refused to even speculate on his meaning. She would remain calm. Apparently he found some sick sort of pleasure in riling her. "I have no definite plans," she admitted. She felt as desolate as her voice sounded. "I was going to be married. I have my teacher's certificate, and someday I may apply to teach P. E. somewhere."

"Then you haven't made any plans for the fall?"

She shook her head. "It doesn't matter. I can work in my father's office or volunteer at the hospital for a while. Gran said the health club isn't doing well, so I might see what I can do there."

Even as she mentioned them, none of her options held any

appeal. The health club that Gramps had left Gran had been an investment and a worthwhile place for his grandkids to hang out, he'd said. Shelly had spent much of life doing just that. Now, Katrina and Betsy were too busy, Trevor lived in Hawaii, Don was gone. . .

She spoke as honestly as she could. "I don't know about my future."

"All right," Trevor said decisively. "We'll take one step at a time. Now—"

"Really, Trevor," Shelly interrupted. "Since when have you become my guardian?"

She watched his face as he pretended thoughtfulness, then straightened and gave her a sidelong look. "I think the first time was when you were about three years old and I was eleven. You were chasing Katrina when you tripped and fell. I put a bandage over your skinned knee—that one right there, to be exact."

"That one?" she asked with feigned innocence as if his finger had not come quite close to touching her knee.

"Exactly," he returned, amusement playing on his lips. "It made it all well again. So," he added, "that makes at least eighteen years total."

"Self-appointed, uninvited guardian?" she quipped. "How could you expose yourself to that?"

"I've often asked that of myself." He pretended to be miserable. "You've always been such a spoiled brat."

"I was not!" she protested.

"You still are," he replied.

Shelly didn't know if it was because the moon went behind a cloud or if the night simply darkened—the despair of life overwhelmed her. "I wish I were just a bratty kid again. I wish I could go back. That time could stand still. I wish. . ." To keep from giving in to the misery, she stood and took a few steps away from him.

Then he was in front of her, his hands gently resting on her shoulders. Pain shrouded his eyes, and she did not shrink from him when he pulled her close.

"It'll be all right," he whispered beside her ear, and she felt that he was telling himself too. Don was his brother. Trevor had loved him. Perhaps as he said she *was* a spoiled brat who thought too often of her own feelings.

Just as she was about to give in to the warmth of his strong, protective arms, he moved back. "You have nothing in particular to do this summer?"

She shook her head. "Mom and Dad mentioned a Caribbean cruise, but that really doesn't interest me."

"What would you like to do?" he asked, his eyes searching hers. She felt he wanted her to say something in particular. But there wasn't anything. What could she say? *Get away. Forget. Pass the time.* She shrugged helplessly.

"I know something that might interest you. The island—"

"Are you inviting my family?" Her words interrupted him. In the past he'd invited her and her parents to his home on the island of Oahu. They had gone, but Shelly never had.

"No. Just you."

"Why would you want me to go away. . .with you?" she asked, her question sounding like an accusation.

"I want to show you something."

Eyeing him suspiciously, she laughed ironically. "It must really be something."

"The most precious thing we have," he said seriously.

She lifted her chin. "And what is that?"

"Life," he said, and something strange glimmered in his eyes.

"I don't have to leave North Carolina to experience life," she said icily.

"No," he agreed. "But you have to go somewhere to see it in its entirety. You've known one man, one lifestyle, one tiny little part of the world, and at twenty-one, you're ready to give up on it."

"Why on earth would you want me with you, Trevor?" she asked suspiciously. "You and I don't even like each other."

"Is that right?" he asked. "Who ever said that I don't like you?"

Shelly sighed and looked up at the stars before again meeting his fathomless eyes. "You've said it in a million ways, Trevor. With a look or a snort or by walking out of a room. It's your attitude, I guess. It's obvious." She turned, her long hair swinging out from her head like a fan. She hurried up the sidewalk.

Neither of them said anything during the fast walk to the car. She got in and slammed the door. After Trevor maneuvered the car out of the parking lot and into the street, Shelly took a deep breath, then began.

"Trevor," she said. "I realize it would be ideal if the entire Landon and Steinbord families could be on good terms. However, where you and I are concerned, that has never happened. I think it's you who need to face reality. I will not go to Hawaii or anywhere else with you."

"As usual," he accused, "you didn't hear me out. I don't recall mentioning the word 'Hawaii.' Even so—would a Hawaiian vacation be so unappealing?"

The car slowed. They had reached the dorm. Trevor switched off the engine, then sat like a stone, as silent and as grim.

Suddenly, Shelly had an awful thought. Her head swung toward him. "You were joking about that, weren't you Trevor?" Oh dear. He must have been. How could she have thought he would invite just her. . .anywhere?

"I have this terrific sense of humor, Shelly, or hadn't you noticed?" He stared straight ahead, tapping the steering wheel as if irritated.

"Not that I believe you were serious," she said, trying to redeem herself. "But if you were, the fact remains that you and I do not communicate on the same level. We've never had what I call a conversation, and when it's attempted, it turns into a disaster. Like tonight."

His head turned toward her. "Tonight was a disaster?"

"Well. . ." she stammered. "Look at us. We're. . .fighting."

"Not we, Shelly," he corrected. "You!"

Without another word, Shelly stormed out of the car and marched into her dorm, wishing she could slam the electronically controlled security door behind her.

❧

Trevor watched her hurry away from him, like she'd done all her life. When she was out of sight he felt like a rose-colored cloud had turned gray. Nothing had changed. For Shelly, anyway. But he'd touched her tonight—something he'd never done before. He'd felt her in his arms, not just in his imagination, not just in the fantasies that he turned into fiction and made into scenes for his books.

He reached into the glove compartment and took out a small notebook and pen. Forcing his thoughts from reality into fiction, he began to write—not as the evening had happened, but as his imaginary hero, James, related to the heroine, Eileen. Doing what he instructed beginning students to do, he stopped writing when the emotions no longer flowed through his fingers and onto the page. He snapped the notebook closed. Inspiration had left him—left him alone with his thoughts. James and Eileen were relegated to their resting place in the glove compartment.

With a deep sigh, Trevor started the engine. For twenty-one years he had warned himself, reprimanded himself, lectured himself, told himself, "Shelly Landon can never be yours, Trevor Steinbord." He'd steeled himself against her—against his own emotions—and even now, he dared not hope. But deep inside churned a smoldering longing for Shelly.

Trevor Steinbord loved Shelly Landon.

He had loved her as much as an eight-year-old boy could love from the moment he stood with his mother in the Landon's nursery and he looked at the dark-haired beauty in her bassinet, surrounded by pink and white, sucking on her tiny thumb. He'd never seen anything so perfect, so beautiful, so inspiring, and he reached out to discover for himself if the infant was real. Shelly's mother said, "Don't touch her little head because of the soft spot."

But Shelly Landon had touched the soft spot of his heart. He'd watched her and protected her when she was a baby and a toddler and his younger brother's best friend. He'd tried not to watch her when she ran through his house as a teenager and was falling in love with his brother, Don.

He'd known that the power of such unrequited, impossible love could be devastating or motivating, so he used it as the dominant theme of his first book. The novel became a bestseller. Everyone who knew him, knew of his love for Shelly. . . except his brother—and Shelly.

There'd always been that necessary distance between him and Shelly—particularly when she was a girl and he a man. Now Shelly was growing into a woman, and Don wasn't between them anymore. But Don's memory was.

Trevor knew he didn't have a chance unless he could find a way for Shelly to put her memories in proper perspective and understand why she didn't like him.

Maybe, if she would accept his island invitation. . .

&

The lobby, stairway, and halls were empty, and no voices sounded from any room. No doubt she had the entire dorm to herself. After reaching her room, Shelly removed the corsage and took the lavender ribbon from the orchid. The flower was beautiful.

She took a pen from the desk, sat down, and inscribed the date, occasion, and name of her escort on the lavender ribbon, then stared at it. She had written, "Trevor Steinbord." There'd never been anyone in her life except Don. She thought of her numerous scrapbooks filled with mementos, newspaper clippings, ribbons from corsages—all of which bore Don's name. A great shudder wracked her body. There would never be anyone else. She laid her head on her arms and cried.

After her sobs subsided, Shelly reminded herself that Trevor had said everything would be all right, and she tried to believe it. To dispel the depression of loneliness, she took off her dress, hung it in the closet, and then soaked in a hot bath. Later, clad in cotton pajamas, she tried unsuccessfully to read, then turned up the radio to drown out the voices as students returned from the dance.

When Peggy came in, Shelly was sitting in the middle of her bed, surrounded by her scrapbooks filled with memories.

"Boy, he really set the place agog, Shelly," Peggy exclaimed. "It's a good thing you got him out of there."

"What? Who?" Shelly asked, astounded.

"Trevor Steinbord! Who else? I mean, it's not often a handsome, famous, older man comes to a college dance."

"Famous?" She laughed.

"Well, he's a famous writer. Some of the students have even read his books. I've heard his stories change people's lives and everything."

"He's not famous, Peggy. Writing is his job. It's not some mantle that has fallen on him. He's just a. . ." she shrugged and kindly added, "just a person."

"Just a person!" Peggy shrieked.

Shelly moved the scrapbook over so Peggy could see pictures of Don. "You can look at these pictures and still make a fuss over Trevor?"

Peggy's face took on a helpless expression. "I'd just better keep quiet, Shelly. I wouldn't want to make you cry."

"Well," Shelly admitted. "I suppose if you compare him with the other guys around here. . ." She glanced over and smiled. "John excluded of course. Compared with the others, Trevor might seem rather special. But to me, he's an older brother who has always been somewhat of a pain, if you know what I mean."

"That kind of pain I could learn to live with," Peggy quipped as she stood. "John and I think it's too early to call it a night, Shelly. I'll be back later—unless you'd like me to stay here with you? I know it's been a rough day."

Peggy had been a wonderful friend through everything. Shelly smiled at her. "I'm fine, Peggy. Go on." Her voice broke, and she turned her attention to the scrapbooks.

"I just wondered, Shelly," Peggy said thoughtfully. "Why would Trevor spend so much time here just to take you out for an hour?"

Shelly stared up at her. "An hour?" Something caught in her throat. "But. . .we did walk around awhile afterwards. And. . . he had to be here to speak at the ceremony."

"That was earlier," Peggy replied. "He could have left before dinner, and no one would have thought ill of him. Why should he hang around at a dinner with a bunch of college students?"

Shelly remembered how she had stormed out of the car without even saying good night. She should have been kinder, or spent a little more time, or at least not argued with him. But no, it wouldn't have worked. And it wasn't as if he had asked to take her out. They had been thrown together. So he wasn't to blame either. He'd worn a tux, borrowed his father's car, and what on earth could he reply when his parents would inevitably ask, "How'd it go, Son?"

"I didn't even say thank you," Shelly realized aloud.

"Shelly," Peggy said, in a reprimanding tone.

Shelly looked at the clock. "He may not be home yet."

"But he may."

She shook her head and hugged her arms, feeling suddenly chilled. "I can't."

"He's hurting too, Shelly," Peggy said softly. "He's making an effort at going on. The way you've described things to me, his family is very close. This can't be easy for them. You could at least make one tiny effort. Can't you put aside your battle with him long enough to say a simple word of gratitude for an effort on your behalf?"

Shelly was stung by her words, but they also had the ring of truth. Peggy smiled and her eyes pleaded with Shelly to understand. After Peggy left the room, Shelly knew her friend meant well. And she was right. Despite her differences with Trevor and that confusing invitation of his, there existed such things as courtesy and decency.

The Steinbords' telephone number was permanently engraved upon her mind. She'd called it millions of times in the past. It was late. She might wake the Steinbords. Trevor might not be home.

She'd hang up if the phone wasn't answered on the first ring.

"That was quick," she said hesitantly.

"Shelly?" His voice held an urgency. "What's up? Are you all right?"

"Yes, Trevor."

"Good. Um, what's on your mind?"

"Were you sitting on the phone?"

"It's by my bed."

"Oh, are you reading?"

"I'm writing."

"What about?"

He laughed. "It's a long story."

"Oh. Well, I just wanted to say thank you."

After a brief silence, he asked, "Thank you?"

"You're making it difficult, Trevor." She felt nervous.

"All right, Shelly. Tell me why you're thanking me."

She cleared her throat, and before she could think of the right words, he continued. "Is it because you had such a wonderful evening? Or was it the orchid that touched your heart? The dinner? The pleasant walk along the lake? Our stimulating conversation? Was it all that, Shelly, or just my delightful company you enjoyed so much?

"I. . .thought you were trying to be kind to me," she said, shaking with indignation. She should have known better than to call.

"Who put you up to this?" he asked.

She inhaled deeply. "Peggy. That's who. It wasn't my idea."

He laughed then. "Ah, Shelly. Thanks for the effort. I know how you feel about me. I'd rather have your honest dislike of me than any pretended politeness."

"I'm sorry I said thank you," she shouted. "And that's not pretended. I'm sorry I called. I'm sorry I had a moment of weakness and thought there was a kind bone in your body. And I'm not being polite either."

"Good." He sounded indifferent. "Good night, Shelly."

He hung up.

She stared at the phone.

He actually hung up on her. Then a thought formed in her mind. Wouldn't it serve him right if she told his family, and hers, that Trevor had invited her to visit him in Hawaii without them!

A chuckle formed in her throat. Yes! If she did that, Trevor Steinbord would have to do some tall explaining to an awful lot of people.

five

Shock. Total, utter, complete shock.

That's what Shelly felt when she looked at the contents of an envelope that came in the mail from Miami. The cover letter began: "Mr. Trevor Steinbord asked that we send the enclosed information. . . ."

To ensure that her mind wasn't playing tricks, she spread out the contents on the bed for a closer inspection. This information was all about a project called Summer Outreach. Volunteers went throughout the world, helping to build schools, medical clinics, churches, or working with organizations that helped the needy.

Suddenly it all made sense. She didn't need a vacation that simply offered more time to indulge her grief. She needed a way to concentrate on something other than the fact that she had expected to be planning a wedding after graduation.

Before another hour had passed, she had devoured the contents of the envelope. The application included was for workers to build a school in Haiti. News clips of a country torn apart by war and poverty flashed through her mind.

This was the first time anything had sparked her real interest in a long time, and she knew exactly what she wanted to do during the summer.

She called Trevor.

He answered on the second ring.

"You were slower this time," she said. "And I hope I woke you."

"Sorry to disappoint you, Shelly, but I wasn't sleeping, just concentrating on a concept I was trying to relate to this blank sheet of paper. Now, to what do I owe this pleasure?"

"You play games with me, Trevor Steinbord!"

"What on earth do you mean, Shelly Landon?" he asked, a trace of humor in his voice.

"You deliberately tempted me with the idea of an island vacation—"

"You were tempted?" he interrupted.

"Well, not really," she demurred, glad he couldn't see her suddenly warm face. "That's just a figure of speech. Anyway, you knew good and well I would never choose a summer of leisure once I looked at those brochures about Haiti. Now admit it."

He paused before he answered her. "I'm never positive about how you might react, Shelly. But about the project. What do you think?"

This was the first time she hadn't resented Trevor's interference or his tendency to act like a parent or a know-it-all big brother to her. "I think it's perfect for me. You knew that, didn't you?"

"I know it was for me, Shelly," he said, his voice growing deep and serious. "I became part of the project right out of college and have been affiliated with it in some form or other for the past ten years."

She hadn't known that. But she remembered something about his having been in Haiti before. She hadn't given it any thought, for she was quite young at the time and later grew accustomed to his being in one foreign country after another.

"Then you were recruiting me!"

"That's one way of putting it," Trevor admitted.

"I like the idea, Trevor. I really do. But. . .it's past the deadline for applications."

"I can get you in," he quickly assured her.

"Then do!"

"If you want me to, I'll talk to your parents about it and make the arrangements. You concentrate on your finals, and I'll get official confirmation back to you as soon as possible. Don't bother with the application."

Shelly wasn't sure why, but she did something she'd never

done before. She said "Thanks" and "Good night," to—of all people—Trevor Steinbord!

෨

Within a few days of Shelly's conversation with Trevor, a letter arrived with a Miami postmark.

With an uncertain fluttering in her stomach, she tore it open and read the brief message. It began by addressing her informally.

> *Dear Shelly,*
> *This is to confirm your acceptance for working with Summer Outreach on our Haiti project. Please complete and return the enclosed form so that we may know either the exact time to expect you or to meet you at the airport.*
> *Pay particular attention to the dress code. You may skip the section asking for reference letters. Since Mr. Steinbord so highly recommended you, we know you will be a tremendous asset to our project.*
> *Looking forward to seeing you the first week in June. We consider ourselves blessed to have you coming aboard.*
>
> *Your friend in Christ,*
> *Paul R. Sinclair*

Blessed? Shelly questioned. *In my state of mind, I'd probably spoil things for anyone as high-spirited as the letter writer sounds.*

Suddenly feeling uncertain, she put the correspondence aside and concentrated on her finals. She still hadn't sent the forms a couple nights later when her family dined with the Steinbords to discuss the upcoming venture and graduation.

"Maybe I shouldn't go away this summer after all." She looked at Gran. "Didn't you say the health club was barely holding its own financially?"

When Gran nodded, Shelly smiled. "If you need me, I'll stay. As you know, I've just about *lived* in that place."

"Thank you, Shelly," Gran said kindly. "But I'm not that concerned about making a profit, and I've never taken a personal interest in it. For now, I think it's best you get away."

Gran's smile trembled and she looked down at her plate. It had been Gran who had told her right after the funeral, "Stay close to us, Shelly. We need you even more, now that Don's gone."

Shelly quickly turned to her parents. "Maybe I should take you up on that Caribbean cruise," she suggested.

Her mother shook her head as if she wouldn't hear of it, and her father, whom she'd always felt was overly protective, was now shoving her out. "As much as we'd like to have you with us, Kitten, we believe this will be better for you at this time. You'll have specific responsibilities to occupy your time and mind."

After dinner, they gathered in the living room and she was given her what Betsy called "graduation/going-away presents."

She laughed upon seeing the designer jeans Katrina gave her, along with a note on a card saying, *Have a great summer!*

"Do you know what the dress code is for Haiti?" Shelly asked.

"Jeans, I heard," Katrina said, puzzled.

Shelly nodded. "Old jeans. The emphasis was on *old*. Anything we take should be able to be torn up or thrown away."

"Well, wear them in Miami," Katrina suggested.

"Perfect!" Shelly said. "Thanks. And of course I'll wear them often here at home. It's just that *this summer* has me a little worried."

Margo jumped in. "There's nothing to worry about, Shelly. Otherwise, Trevor would never have suggested this project."

"And he knows he has to take good care of you," Hanlan interjected, "or answer to all of us."

"There's not even a question about that, Hanlan," Margo

said, sounding like a typical mother defending her son's integrity.

"You might not know it," Shelly began hesitantly, "but Trevor and I never hit it off. . .exactly. I mean, with his being older. . .and away a lot." They were all staring at her. She smiled weakly.

"Yes, we do know that, Shelly," Margo replied.

Everything grew strangely quiet, like it always did when she mentioned Trevor. Nobody ever offered information about him either. Talking about Trevor in this house was like going to the bathroom. It was a personal, private matter—something one just didn't discuss.

"Here, open my present next," Betsy said, breaking the tension. It was a travel kit for makeup. Gran gave her a generous gift certificate from her boutique.

Shelly already knew what her parents' present was, since she wouldn't be taking a Caribbean cruise. They'd told her that Trevor said he would take care of her expenses, but the information in the manila envelope said that participants would pay their own and outlined how some worked to meet expenses and some were sponsored by churches, family, and friends. "We'll pay all your expenses," her dad had said, and her mother had readily agreed.

When Margo and Hanlan presented her with a set of luggage, Shelly gasped. "I thought the pink gown was my graduation present from you," she said, overwhelmed.

"Nancy said you could use some luggage," Margo explained with a smile.

"Sounds like you people are eager to get rid of me," Shelly accused. "And at the same time you make it difficult for me to want to leave."

"We just want what's best for you, Shelly," her father said, a suspicious moisture covering his eyes.

❧

Two days after graduation, Shelly arrived at the airport in Miami and was met by a young woman about her own age, holding a white poster-board sign with SUMMER OUTREACH written in bold black magic-marker letters. Shelly, wearing her designer jeans, went to her immediately, and they retrieved Shelly's bags filled mainly with old clothes.

As the small van lumbered along the highway beneath a clear blue sky, Shelly and the young woman, Cristy, became acquainted.

"What's the program like?" Shelly finally asked when there was a lull in their comparing the flat stretches of land and water with high mountain ranges.

"I only work in the Miami office," Cristy said. "So I'll leave those details to your leaders."

Shelly nodded but thought Cristy wore a strange little grin, and the girl's sidelong glance reminded Shelly of a look Trevor often wore—one of knowing some secret that he wasn't going to share.

Cristy drove to the university in Miami, and Shelly promptly wondered if she was too old for this project since she'd been assigned a dorm room with a girl just out of high school. However, the girl's excitement over Shelly's having been a cheerleader and having graduated from college renewed some of Shelly's better memories, and she soon forgot the age difference.

The next morning, after the group gathered in the dining hall for breakfast and orientation, Shelly realized what a big organization this was.

"Good morning," sounded over a speaker. Heads turned to find the source. "I'm on my soapbox, so that's a signal for you to listen," a man said good-naturedly. Shelly was close enough to the food line to see the man with a microphone standing on a low crate turned upside down. Conversation died down, and the man introduced himself as Paul Sinclair, a history professor at the university who donated his summers to the organization.

The one who wrote the letter, Shelly thought.

In jeans and a short-sleeved knit shirt, he looked as friendly and informal as his letter had sounded. He appeared young to be a professor, but upon closer scrutiny she saw that his dark brown hair was sprinkled with gray at the temples. His demeanor was youthful, however, and Shelly immediately felt at ease. He explained that after general orientation, the large groups would be broken up into smaller groups and they would go their separate ways for a three-week training session. After that, the groups would depart for places all over the U.S. and abroad to help in almost every conceivable job.

Soon, they broke up into smaller groups, and Shelly's young dorm-mate separated from her. Shelly's group consisted of forty young people, besides staff and instructors. Two married couples would be in charge, along with Paul Sinclair.

He reminded them that their positions were strictly voluntary. "The work in Haiti will be hard," he said. "Their country has been devastated by war and their emotions by personal loss."

Shelly bit her lip at that remark, feeling that terrible sinking feeling each time she thought of her own recent loss. She forced her attention back to the speaker.

"Not everyone is able to adapt to the situation. If you decide it's not for you, we have plenty of positions right here in Miami that are just as important, though not as physically demanding."

He asked for questions. One eager young man said, "I'm ready—had all my shots. Now what?"

"Boot Camp!" Paul Sinclair said with a grin.

"Boot Camp?" the boy questioned.

"The Lord's Boot Camp," came Paul Sinclair's reply. "And it's tough."

six

Shelly felt he had probably exaggerated, but she quickly changed her mind after arriving on Merritt Island, a small barren place with only a few scraggly palms and twisted trees. There they set up their tents, dining area, equipment, and office station.

By the time dawn touched the sky, they had already rolled out of their tents for calisthenics, followed by devotions led by Paul. He gave an opportunity for anyone to speak from the heart.

Most of the group were between eighteen and twenty-two years old; however, several members were in their thirties, a couple were in their forties, and one spry, muscular man was sixty-eight. Whenever an ability or talent was mentioned, Paul assigned jobs. Shelly's would be to help with morning exercises.

Scott, a hazel-eyed, sandy-haired young man enthusiastically related his joy at being part of the group for the summer. He planned to enter seminary in the fall and wanted to become a minister of music and work with youth.

"Looks like we have our song leader," Paul said and asked Scott to lead them. Scott taught them several songs he had used with young children in his church.

After a prayer, Paul closed with the admonition that they contemplate on a particular verse of Scripture each day.

Then the work began, and there were still two hours to go before breakfast! There was oral instruction on carpentry, foundation digging, cement mixing, block laying, building squaring, and roof nailing. Then there was on-the-job training.

Paul, who worked along with them on erecting a small building and gave instructions asked, "Well, what do you think?"

The group looked it over. "It's a little dilapidated," Shelly admitted, looking from the make-shift building toward her tentmates, Jill and Teresa, who agreed.

"That's all right," Paul assured them, his lips spreading in a wide smile over straight white teeth. "We'll tear it apart and put it together again tomorrow."

"You wouldn't," Shelly protested, and even good-natured Scott groaned.

"That's how we do it," Paul replied, his brown eyes glinting in the sun. "Practice makes perfect!"

And for three weeks, that's what they did. Practice. Build. Tear apart. Rebuild. Although Shelly had found cheerleading to be strenuous and exhausting, this work touched muscles she hadn't known she had.

She was grateful to Scott, who soon had them singing laughable little ditties when the work became grueling—like when they nailed together tin roofs in the hottest part of the day.

After trying to cool themselves by drinking hot Kool-Aid, it was a blessed relief the day the clouds burst. They all stood in the rain, their faces lifted toward the heavens and their mouths open for the cool liquid. Upon discovering that their pond-washed clothes that hung on a line stretched from tree to tree had fallen into the mud, they simply made the mess complete by laughing and playing in the mud themselves. Afterward, they bathed in the pond.

The women laughed and splashed around in the pond in their bathing suits. "So this is why they insisted we buy soap that floats," Shelly said as she tried to wash her hair and hold onto her soap while kicking her feet to keep her head above water.

Each night, just before falling asleep almost as soon as her body fell into the sleeping bag, she realized anew the value of the verses of the day, such as, "Come unto me, all ye that labour and are heavy laden, and I will give you rest."

After three weeks of isolation on the island, it felt strange to return to civilization. Their group had developed a sense of peace and the unity that comes from joining together for a common purpose. It was a good feeling, and Shelly found herself looking forward to the rest of the summer in Haiti.

While the staff was in a meeting, the workers went out to buy whatever personal items they needed. Later they were each issued three sets of clothing they would wear during their work in Haiti.

That afternoon the group, dressed in jeans and T-shirts with the words SUMMER OUTREACH emblazoned across the front, waited to board the chartered plane to Haiti.

Shelly was talking with Jill, Teresa, and Scott when she saw the blond head of Trevor Steinbord as he walked up and began talking with some of the staff. A sudden wave of loss invaded her being, and she turned from the stabbing pain of his resemblance to Don. She realized, gratefully, that there hadn't been time to think of anything but work during the past three weeks.

Soon, she was ascending the steps to the plane. She followed Jill into the coach section and had just settled herself in an aisle seat when a flight attendant approached her.

"Shelly Landon?"

"Yes," Shelly replied, surprised.

"A gentleman in first class would like to see you."

"All right," Shelly answered, wondering what she'd done wrong or what kind of unexpected chore they had in mind now!

As soon as she entered first class, she saw him. Gentleman, indeed! Trevor Steinbord. Sitting, watching her as she made her way up the aisle toward him in all her grunginess. He looked immaculate in creased lightweight slacks and a white shirt open at the neck. Beside him on the seat were a suit coat and tie. "Sit down, Shelly," he said.

Following his gesture, she sat across from Trevor on a long seat, separated by a narrow table. Paul and one of the married couples sat across the aisle from them in a similar seating arrangement. They smiled at her, but she sensed a curiosity in their eyes as they glanced from her to Trevor.

Shelly fastened her seatbelt, then looked out the window at the airport, runways, scenery, and movement of baggage.

As the plane began to taxi down the runway, Trevor asked casually, "How's it going, Shelly?"

She met his eyes in a direct stare. "Well, I haven't had a bath, a real bath, in three weeks. No makeup. Stiff hair." She held out her long braid. "No decent clothes. I've never looked so awful in my life." She leaned toward him. "You seem to always see me uncomfortable and at my worst, don't you?"

"You look fine. The smell though. . ." He grimaced, then his low chuckle turned into a full-fledged laugh. "I'm teasing, Shelly!"

As soon as they were airborne and the "fasten seatbelt" signs blinked off, Trevor opened his briefcase, then brought out a piece of paper and laid it on the table. He took a pen from the inside pocket of his suit coat that lay on the seat beside him.

Shelly looked at the paper and saw that it had Summer Missions letterhead. So, Trevor must be one of the executives. Why did he want her in here if he were going to sit and write, she wondered.

After a moment, he looked up and smiled at Shelly's curious stare. "Have you written to your parents, Shelly?" he asked.

"I called them last night," she said stiffly.

"I promised Mom and Dad I would write to them the minute I saw you and let them know how you're doing." His expression became solemn, and his eyes bored into hers. "How are you really doing, Shelly?"

The abrupt question and mesmerizing blue gaze caught her off guard. She would have given a glib answer, but she knew he was serious. Still, she didn't want to explore her deep-seated feelings. She was here to overcome them or, better yet, forget they'd ever existed.

She was grateful for the flight attendant who came then and

stood at the end of the table, offering drinks. "Oh, yes. Thank you," Shelly said, blinking away unwanted thoughts and concentrating on the clear, sparkling liquid in the plastic cup.

"Well, Trevor," she said lightly, after taking a sip and setting the cup on the table. "I'm doing great. I've learned a lot in three weeks. How to appreciate bath tubs. And air-conditioning!" She hugged her arms to herself, shivering slightly, but said with determination, "I'm not going to complain, but it would be nice if I could bottle this cool air and take it with me. I have a feeling Haiti will be as hot as Florida."

Seeing Trevor's pleasant expression, she refused to think of Don, so she babbled on. "And, after all that hot Kool-Aid, I appreciate a simple thing like an ice cube."

She gingerly touched the ice cubes with a finger and watched them bounce back. "Honestly, though," she said in a soft voice, watching the bubbles of her soft drink in the plastic cup. "It's good for me. I know that. I'm part of something good."

After a moment's speculation of her, Trevor continued to write.

"You're not telling your parents what I said." She reached for the sheet and paper and read silently.

> *Dear Mom and Dad,*
> *As promised, I'm writing to let you know about Shelly. She's sitting across from me on the plane. She looks about ten pounds thinner, but it's apparently muscle, for she has a healthy glow on her cheeks, which are considerably browner. She speaks of an appreciation of all the luxuries she has missed. She is none the worse for her three weeks of deprivation, and her eyes reflect a determination to be part of a worthwhile endeavor to reach out to needy humanity.*

Very slowly, as Shelly read, she raised the sheet of paper upward until she hoped it hid her face from Trevor. She wasn't sure if she should laugh, or cry, or deny it, or admit it, or what.

Was Trevor trying to use positive psychology on a young woman who had suffered loss? Was he being sarcastic because she had given him such trite answers to his questions? Was he being a writer, fictionalizing the situation to fit what his parents would want to hear? Was he an older man trying to give purpose to a girl he said had never grown up? Was he being a friend, using irony to make her laugh? Perhaps his expression would tell her.

She lowered the paper and looked at him. He was watching his fingers click his ball-point pen, and his expression told her nothing. Sighing, she placed the paper on the table.

"Well," she began, as if that over-written paragraph were serious, "if I accomplished all that in three weeks, I wonder what is in store for me in Haiti."

"Whatever is in you," he replied immediately, meeting her eyes.

"Don't you know what's in me, Trevor?"

"A vacuum. And the only thing that can fill that emptiness is your grief and anger and disillusionment. There is an aching loneliness. A desolation that says nothing good can again come your way."

It was as if he had looked into her soul and knew her feelings as well, or even better, than she. "I had it all, Trevor," she said, lowering her eyes to the table. "How can I not long for that?"

"No," he said staunchly. She looked at him as he shook his head. "Unless your purpose for living comes from within yourself, you have nothing. That's something we have to find alone. Ourselves with God. No one else must be our purpose for living."

"I know those things," she said, having been taught them all her life. "But they are so much easier to say than to feel."

"I know that," he agreed. "I've had to discover for myself what is in me. Realize the many different paths our lives can take. There is much in us—in you. And I know it's not easy, going on when life deals out its reverses."

"Really, Trevor," she said rather uneasily. "You've always done what you wanted, and you travel anywhere you want."

He seemed ready to change his mind about what he was going to say. "So can you. Whatever you want. All you have to do is decide."

He made it sound so easy. Nothing was that simple, and of course he knew it. "I could use a pillow," she said.

"One pillow coming up," he replied and caught the eye of the flight attendant. "See?" he said after the request was granted.

At least for the moment, the tension dissipated. She took off her tennis shoes, poked the pillow into the corner of the seat, leaned sideways against it, and drew her knees up onto the seat. She did not say anything when Trevor leaned over the table to spread his suit coat over her arms and shoulders.

She caught a whiff of a fantastic cologne and felt the brush of his hands against her shoulders as he adjusted the coat. With eyes tightly squeezed shut, she longed for the nearness of Don. Never again would he be near. How could Trevor even say she could have what she wanted, when all she ever really wanted was Don.

After Trevor returned to his seat, Shelly peered at him through shielded lashes. He was writing. She dozed for a while, enjoying the coziness beneath the suit coat and being lulled by the monotonous hum of the engines. When she opened her eyes again, he was still writing. The only change she detected was that his golden curls looked as if they'd been rumpled by fingers running through them.

"Do you write all the time?" she asked.

"Yes," he replied without looking at her. "When I'm not writing on paper, I'm writing in my mind. I can't even read a book without taking it apart, seeing how the author put it together and if I could or would have done it differently."

"How terrible," she said.

"Terrible?" he laughed. "Writing is my bread and butter, Shelly."

"Is that why you. . .look at everybody so intensely?"

He chuckled. "I don't look. I absorb."

"Well, don't absorb me," she quipped.

Then his eyes met hers, and they held a reflection of the azure sky. She thought the glint of the sun brought a twinkle to them. But she must have been mistaken. Trevor's eyes never twinkled.

"I absorbed you long ago, so your request cannot be honored this time."

"Well, don't put me in your books," she warned. His quirked eyebrows and amused expression prompted another question. "You haven't, have you?"

"You would never recognize yourself, Shelly. Never."

"Which one am I in?" she asked curiously.

He didn't seem to hear her, but he stopped writing and put the notebook and pencil on the table. That moody gray look passed over his eyes as his gaze slowly turned toward the window. That was the Trevor she knew: distant, moody, unapproachable, out of reach.

"I suppose I should return to my seat," she said reluctantly.

He looked at her, and she thought it was perhaps because she made no effort to rise, that his eyes took on his knowing expression. "You may stay here if you like."

Her spirits rose. "Do you suppose Mr. Sinclair would mind?"

"You don't need to worry about that," he replied. "You know, Shelly, this is a volunteer project. You may leave at any time."

She leaned over to the window and looked down at fluffy white clouds floating far between them and the ocean. Her eyes glinted mischievously. "Any time?"

"I would advise that you wait until we land in Haiti."

"And where on earth could I go then?"

"We could send you back home, or if you decide you want a vacation after all, my home in Hawaii is vacant."

He was back to that again. But it was the kind of invitation any Landon or Steinbord would extend to a member of either family. And, too, the words seemed much more acceptable with her sitting there in jeans and a yellow T-shirt with SUMMER MISSIONS printed on it, than they had when she was wearing an evening gown of Parisian pink.

"I'll stick it out," she said.

"You love it, don't you?" he asked quietly.

"Under the circumstances," Shelly replied honestly, "I think it's the best possible thing for me. But I've only been through the training period."

"That's the toughest part, Shelly. Becoming acclimated to hard labor."

"I was already accustomed to that in cheerleading," she countered. "Try doing the double-decker shoulder-stand, drop over, triple flip, and then finish with a Chinese split."

He grimaced. "Just watching you made my blood curdle."

"You watched me?"

"Well," he hedged. "You happened to be in my line of vision as Don ran for his touchdown."

Unable to speak of Don freely, she changed the subject. "What's Haiti like?"

"It's hard to say in a few words," he said after a moment. Then he reached down beside him for a book. "Here, let me read a few lines from this." He turned to the front flap of the book and began to read, bringing vivid descriptions to Shelly's mind of beauty, romance, mystery, poverty, cruelty, kindness, and humor. She could almost hear the crowing of the roosters and the beating of the drums and see coffee growing on the mountainsides, then valleys, bright flowers, dark seas, and gingerbread houses.

Not wanting Trevor to detect the stir of excitement that welled up in her at the description of Haiti, she jested, "Oh, I love good books, Trevor. You will have to let me read that when you're finished."

"Yeah, right!" he said accusingly, knowing she had never read anything he wrote. "Ah," he exclaimed suddenly, when he glanced out the window. "I thought it was about time it came into view. Look! There's Haiti," he said.

She looked down at the land jutting out into the ocean, like a two-pronged fork.

"Port-au-Prince is between the two land masses. Some refer to the shape as an irregular triangle; to me it looks more like a crescent." His face turned toward her. Lightheartedness touched his voice when he added, "Fasten your seat belt, Shelly. We're going to Haiti!"

Strange—his admonition sounded not like an order, but rather like a challenge. Stranger, too, for Trevor to indicate he felt that same sense of adventure that suddenly flooded her. She watched a smile touch his lips as he looked down upon the crescent-shaped Haiti.

Eager to see what lay in store for her in Haiti after they landed, Shelly slipped out into the aisle while Trevor was still gathering his coat and briefcase. The moment she stepped to the doorway of the plane, a blast of hot air hit her face. She stepped back into someone and turned. "Oh, Mr. Sinclair. Excuse me. That heat is shocking after the air-conditioning."

He laughed lightly. "That's something we'll have to warn about next time," he said, then added, "Call me Paul. We'll be working together all summer."

"You may have noticed I'm not all that great with bricks and mortar," she jested.

"Do you mean we might have to send you back to boot camp?" he threatened.

"Heaven forbid!" she gasped, and they laughed.

She longed for the comfort of the distant airport terminal, away from the glaring sun, but found it felt even worse than the outside. The suffocating heat mingled with the odor of human flesh that hadn't had a bath in a while.

Soon, they were all being herded out the front door, and Paul was nearby, saying, "I hope the tap-taps are out there."

"Who are they?" Shelly asked, and Paul laughed.

"They," he said with emphasis, "are our transportation. Ah! There they are."

Shelly looked. Out front stood two vehicles resembling little trolleys or small busses with opened windows. They were painted in vivid rainbow colors. One was being loaded with luggage.

Shelly stood near Paul, talking with Jill and Teresa, while others were climbing aboard the low, narrow busses. A movement caught her eye as a long, black car moved in their direction. *It must have air-conditioning,* Shelly thought, noting the darkened windows were up. It parked behind the luggage tap-tap.

"I'll be in touch, Paul," Trevor was saying, and Shelly turned toward him. He grinned, "Don't work too hard."

She was about to ask, "Aren't you going with us?" but he had already turned, and with his suit coat over one shoulder and his briefcase in his hand, he was striding away from them, down the broken sidewalk. He opened the back door of the black car and put his briefcase and coat in the back seat. When he opened the door on the passenger side, Shelly saw what appeared to be the outline of a woman behind the wheel.

"Who is that?" she asked Paul.

"I don't know, Shelly, but I'm sure Trevor has a lot of friends in Haiti." He took her arm and steered her toward the tap-taps.

Some of the seats faced each other and Paul sat across from her.

"We have a lot to look forward to this summer," he said, settling back against the hard seat.

"Yes," Shelly agreed. "Building a schoolhouse to completion and not having to tear it down."

He laughed as the tap-tap started up noisily.

"By the way," Shelly asked, having to shout to be heard, "what does 'tap-tap' mean?"

"It means 'tap-tap'!" Paul shouted back, hitting on the side of the vehicle. "When a passenger wants to get off, he taps loudly on the side."

They laughed.

Finally, the tap-tap settled down to a mild roar.

"Trevor and I talked this morning, Shelly," Paul said. "He

said you two were acquainted."

"We grew up on the same street," she said. "But at different times."

"Oh, you mean because of the age difference?" he asked, after a thoughtful moment, and she nodded.

"I. . .loved his brother," she replied, then turned her face toward the open window, feeling the burning wind against her cheeks.

"I know how you feel, Shelly," he said. "I know."

Before long, Scott had everyone singing, "I've got the joy, joy, joy, joy, down in my heart. . .And I'm so happy. So very happy. . . ."

Shelly wasn't singing and was only vaguely aware of the dirt yards, tin-roofed houses, and little brown, naked bodies, as the tap-taps rattled toward Port-au-Prince. Soon, she was aware that Paul, too, was gazing silently out the open window.

Knowing he was lost in his thoughts, Shelly studied his face. It was interesting, especially that slight cleft in his chin. His jawline was wide, giving him a look of strength. He had a very nice smile and would be considered good-looking.

Long black lashes closed over his eyes for an instant, in stark contrast to the gray at his temples. Then his eyes opened, and Shelly knew he had purposely allowed her to witness the effect of some disturbing thought that had crossed his mind. She had a feeling that he truly did know how she felt. She was glad. For there was no way she could communicate with those who had only joy in their hearts . . .

She returned his warm smile. Soon, he joined in singing, "I have the love of Jesus, love of Jesus down in my heart. . ."

Yes, Paul, she thought as her head turned again toward the window. *I know. I too have Jesus in my heart. But it will take a while before I can sing about it.*

A horn honked and Shelly saw the long black car ease by their tap-tap on the left. Trevor waved, his golden hair obviously even behind the dark window. Many in the tap-tap waved back. The car pulled away from them and disappeared into the distance.

"You didn't wave," Paul accused, a curious gleam in his eye.

"He wasn't waving at me," she replied innocently. "He knows perfectly well I would never acknowledge anyone riding around in an air-conditioned car on a day like this."

Paul laughed out loud. "Yes, indeed," he said. "I have the feeling this is going to be one of my more challenging summers." A slow grin touched his lips. Shelly smiled at the warmth in his smile and the intensity in his brown eyes.

seven

"Do you think you can finish the book this summer, Trevor?" Carmen asked, as the long, black, air-conditioned car left the tap-tap far behind and sped toward the hills of Montjolie, on the outskirts of Port-au-Prince.

"It's hard to say, Carmen. There've been other things occupying my time and mind since last winter."

She reached over and squeezed his hand in a comforting gesture. His publisher's wife had already expressed her condolences, not only last winter in a telephone call and a handwritten note, but again a short while ago when he'd gotten into the car. Returning her hand to the wheel, she drove onto a narrow road shaded by oaks, pine, cedar, and mahogany. The rich verdure reminded Trevor of the North Carolina mountains that he loved but had felt compelled to leave.

When he'd received word last November that Don was badly hurt, he was in Haiti. His publisher had given him unlimited access to the guest house at his villa so that Trevor could have the solitude so necessary for his best writing. When Trevor learned that Don had been hurt, he knew that Shelly would be in pain. Trevor hurt for them both. He'd been able to get a private plane and fly directly to the States, arriving in North Carolina within hours. He returned to Haiti after the new year, but his heart had been too heavy to write, so he spent much of his time researching Haiti's history and making notes. Haiti had been in its rainy season, and it seemed the gray weather matched the grief of his heart.

Now the rains had ended. Haiti would simmer beneath the summer sun for the next few months, with little rainfall. He caught glimpses of modern homes far back on the hills. Montjolie was a favored residential area of wealthy Haitians and foreign visitors, and Carmen's vacation estate was located there.

Her French villa sprawled lazily on top of the hill, glistening white in the late afternoon sun. She drove around to the guest house at the back of the villa and parked behind a Land Rover.

"I see your transportation is here," Carmen said, pleased that the Jeep had already arrived. Although she offered the use of her car, Trevor liked to have his own transportation.

"Thanks," Trevor smiled as he took his briefcase and coat from the back seat.

"Nona should have everything under control in the guest house. Just let me know if you need anything. I'll have her whip up a supper so come on over as soon as you're settled."

He nodded, tossing the suit coat carelessly over his shoulder. As Carmen drove around the villa, Trevor stood for a moment before entering the guest house. When he'd been here during the rains, he was acutely aware of Haiti's poverty, deprivation, and political problems. Now, he looked at the mango, guava, grapefruit, and orange trees between the villa and the guest house. He rather favored the two mulberry trees next to the guest house and liked the flowering hibiscus on each side of the porch steps. Haiti, in spite of its troubles, had never looked so beautiful to him.

I mustn't allow my imagination to go too far afield, he warned himself.

He looked around as he walked through the living room area and into the dining room that he used as a work area. He opened the desk drawers and saw the papers he had hastily stuffed there before flying to Miami a few days ago.

The drawers were not disturbed during his absence. Nona had been carefully instructed never to touch any of his papers when she cleaned. He put his briefcase on the table and walked into the hallway, past the bathroom, and into the bedroom where he hung his coat in the closet.

After walking back to the bathroom, he saw that the hamper

was empty. Nona would have washed his dirty clothes.

Upon returning to the bedroom, he changed into a pair of walking shorts and a knit short-sleeved shirt and took off the dress shoes and sweaty socks, replacing them with sandals. Then he walked out past the living room and onto the narrow porch that had a view of the sloping hillside, lush with greenery, that dipped into a valley and rose sharply to another peak. On his left was a corner view of Port-au-Prince, but most of that view was obscured by Carmen's villa.

There was no chance of rain now—little chance of even a breeze—so he left the doors and windows open and walked from the porch along the narrow dusty path, onto the cobbled stones leading to the front of the villa.

He ascended the steps of Carmen's verandah and stood for a moment at the concrete wall, looking out upon Port-au-Prince. It was up here, on the hillsides and hilltops, that the wealthy lived. But most of them, in their wealth, helped ease the pain and poverty of the less fortunate. The most recent war had brought them together, for its devastation had scarred rich and poor alike. Few families had escaped the plague of death, and it had brought them closer together, just as Don's death had reconfirmed his own family's closeness. Could it be possible that the pain of death could also bring him and Shelly—?

His thoughts were interrupted by Carmen's arrival. His eyes swept her face which was devoid of makeup. He knew her in Paris as a beautiful woman, elegantly coifed, with perfect clothes for whatever occasion arose for the wife of an important publisher. He had seen her as the perfect hostess at her family's Parisian estate when the invited guests included a film producer that Carmen's husband hoped would be interested in making Trevor's first book into a movie. He had seen her mothering her three children who were entering their teen years. But here she was relaxed, making up for the pressures and tension of running a home and playing hostess to her husband's clients.

"How old is Leon now?" Trevor asked.

"Almost fifteen," she answered with a sigh. "That's a terrible age," she added with a smile, "but then so is thirteen. Emile and Cecile have now entered their teen years. Believe me, I need this vacation."

Trevor nodded, understanding. He gazed out at the dusk settling upon Port-au-Prince. No traffic jams, no sirens, no noisy night life like when he traveled to cities like Los Angeles, New York, and Miami. Strange, how this place of such poverty and need could emit such tranquillity of spirit. There was something noble about those who endured suffering. To whom, or what, he wondered, would the people of Haiti turn now that war had overthrown their dictator and they were being told they must embrace democracy?

"Strange, in the midst of such need, I find my most peaceful moments," Carmen said. "You feel it, too, for it is in those early chapters of your novel."

"Yes, it is the contrast I hope to capture in the book," he said. "In the big cities we long for peace and quiet, yet those cities with all their plenty seem to breed greed, power, and selfishness, while the people in such great need have such gentle spirits. They exhibit a selflessness, a caring, that must come from having endured suffering. It seems to be our needs that bring us to the realization of basic human worth. Life throws us some difficult problems, you know that?"

She smiled up at him. "I know that very well, Trevor," she replied. "There are so many aspects to my life. I need this respite from Paris society and motherhood and even being a wife so that I can be rejuvenated. Antoine needs it too, but in a different way. I need this respite away from the pressures and tensions in order to go back to them with renewed vigor and determination. Antoine needs it to get away, yet he thrives on the pressures of city life and in making a big business work. His world is different from mine. He provides me with all the things that are supposed to make life beautiful and enjoyable, all the luxuries and the pleasantries called the good life. . ." She paused. "And it is that."

Trevor nodded. He knew. He'd been successful by the world's standards for over a decade. But that success had not made him content.

He smiled ruefully as Shelly's image crossed his mind. She was here, in Haiti. With chagrin, he wondered how he might find a way to make her see him as a human being and perhaps come to like him. She had tolerated him upon occasion—like in the plane when they'd flown from Miami to Haiti—but of course, she couldn't very well have run away while thousands of miles high in the air.

For an instant, he soared with hope and anticipation. He had no guarantees that Shelly would ever like him, much less learn to love her. But as long as she was free from commitment to any other man, he would do his best to win her love.

❧

After the dusty thirty-minute ride from the airport to Port-au-Prince, the mission group stayed in a dorm at the Bible Institute for the night.

"Running water and a real bathroom!" Shelly squealed delightedly to Jill, who was already heading for one of the stalls in the long room where all the women piled in for hot showers. It wasn't quite as luxurious as the university dorm, but still smarting from three weeks on Merritt Island, the cleansing soap and water felt like paradise.

After showers, the group gathered in the dining hall where dark-skinned young people were scurrying in and out of the kitchen and around various food and drink stations. All the girls wore white blouses and navy skirts; the boys wore white short-sleeved shirts and navy pants.

They were supervised by an older couple. Paul introduced the man as Pastor Zabute and asked him to say grace. The pastor prayed a long, fervent prayer, expressing his gratitude for the group who had come to help his people, then asked God's blessings on the food.

The group helped themselves to the food as they walked

through the serving line. They were relieved to find the food looked familiar. Golden fried plantains and rice mixed with peas sent up tantalizing aromas. Although carrots mixed with sliced beets seemed a tad unusual, only a few passed them up. Everyone took thick chunks of the meat.

"What kind of meat is this?" Jill asked Shelly, after she took the first bite.

Shelly chewed thoughtfully. "Steak, I guess," she said and shrugged. "It's a little chewy, but it tastes good."

"Wrong," said Tim, a fellow team member sitting across the table from them. He grinned mischievously.

She grimaced. "Don't tell me it's dog meat!"

"Or cat!" Jill whispered, shrilly. "I'll make a spectacle of myself right here."

"Nope," Tim said smugly. "Iguanas eat the dogs and cats."

Shelly look askance at the meat. "This is. . .iguana?" The thought of eating iguana didn't bother her—it was the thought of the iguana eating dogs and cats that did.

"Nope!"

"Well, what is it then?"

"Do you like it?"

She had, but now that he asked, she wondered. "It's. . . okay."

"Tell you later," he said.

She and Jill looked skeptically at the meat, but seeing that neither Tim nor anyone else seemed to have a problem with it, they ate it.

After the young people took the empty plates and brought the dessert, Tim revealed his secret. "Goat meat," he said.

"Oh," Shelly gestured nonchalantly, "only a goat!" She swallowed hard, casting a sidelong glance at Jill. "Well, I don't suppose that's any worse than a cow or a pig," She moved the dessert dish closer and after only the minutest of inspections with her spoon, she tackled the dessert, a fresh fruit salad.

After dinner, Paul introduced the Haitian people seated at his table, and each spoke a few words of gratitude to the mission team. In some cases, the Haitians spoke French and Paul translated their words into English for the volunteers. Other than the minister and his wife, the Haitians were all school officials and their wives. Once the greetings had ended, Paul reminded the group that they would get up at six o'clock the next morning.

A few groans sounded, but everyone knew what to expect, and one person said, "Boot Camp, here we come again!"

"It's not as hard as Boot Camp," Tim said. "I've been on a project like this before. You will work hard, but the satisfaction is greater."

Satisfaction, Shelly thought early the next morning when a loud rapping sounded on the dorm door and Melanie called for her and Jill to rise and shine.

"We're up!" Shelly called as her legs swung around and her feet hit the floor. "Come on, Jill. It's time to get started on our summer of satisfaction."

❧

During the next week, Shelly was too busy to think. After devotions and breakfast that first morning, they loaded onto the tap-taps and made their way to the barren site of the future schoolhouse, outside a small village about thirty minutes from Port-au-Prince. The site was a fenced-in area a short distance from Pastor Zabute's church. At 8:00 A.M., children, all dressed alike, pledged allegiance to the flag that flew outside, then filed into the church for their schooling. Others, wearing different colors signifying their schools, walked toward the village.

The team set up tents and had the same tentmates as during Boot Camp. Shelly felt physically exhausted after that first day of work. In the middle of the night, she awoke to strange sounds.

"What is that?" she whispered softly, in case the others weren't awake.

"I think it's drums," one girl said.

"Sounds like a weird kind of flute," offered Teresa.

"It's eerie," Jill said. "I heard that many of these people

practice voodoo or worship the devil."

"Then we'd better claim that Bible verse we learned in Boot Camp," Shelly said more bravely than she felt. "Greater is He that is in you, than he that is in the world."

They grew silent, but the next morning, they admitted that none of them had slept soundly. After staggering through their second day of work, they resolved they had to trust the Lord and get their rest.

Each morning at six, they crawled out of the tents and worked until 8:00 A.M. Then they stopped for breakfast. After eating, they worked until noon, when they had an hour for lunch and Bible study. They were required to learn a Bible verse every day—and live by it. The first day's verse was "Work as unto the Lord, and not as unto men."

"Paul was clever to give us that verse," Jill exclaimed as she stretched on her sleeping bag. "Nobody could do this only for man!" Shelly and the two other tentmates agreed, but none really complained. In spite of the fatigue, they were on an emotional and spiritual high.

As the week wore on, the heat intensified. They wore caps to shield their faces. Fingernails broke and hands became rough and skinned. The workers guzzled water, and although they had all had typhoid, tetanus, and diphtheria shots, they drank only bottled water. Even with their precautions about the water and food preparation, some workers got "Haitian happiness" and had to periodically run for the outhouse.

Every day small children and some adults gathered outside the fence to watch them work. Scott sometimes led the group in singing familiar hymns in English, and the group outside the fence joined in Creole.

Haitian men, women, and young people helped too. One of the Haitian men was in charge of making concrete, and others helped carry it. Almost everything was done by hand. The workers passed buckets of mortar and concrete. Members of the local church lent their support by hauling barrels of water from the river.

There was a tremendous sense of satisfaction each afternoon at four o'clock when the day's work was done.

On Saturday they were free to go into town, sightsee, or just rest. Shelly, her tentmates, along with Tim and Scott, were glad Paul joined them, for he spoke French fluently and was able to communicate with the villagers who spoke Creole. Shelly realized how inadequate her four semesters of college French were, but was surprised at how many words and phrases she was able to understand and speak brokenly.

The people knew why the mission group was there, and they were friendly and had gentle manners. Shelly was thrilled with their sweet natures. Only one person concerned her: sitting in front of a store was a tall, skinny guy who draped his leg and foot around his neck and smoked a cigarette with his toes.

"He's harmless," Paul assured them, "just limber."

On Sunday, Pastor Zabute conducted worship services in Creole. He again expressed his elation at the Summer Outreach group being in the area. He had wanted to have the school for many years but had to go through the time-consuming, painstaking process of gaining the necessary permissions. Each Sunday morning the front rows of long, backless benches were reserved for Summer Outreach personnel. Pastor Zabute was not concerned about schedules. He preached until he finished!

No one minded, however, for each needed the spiritual rejuvenation his sermons provided. After evening vespers, everyone went to bed early.

Late that first Sunday night, as Shelly looked up through the high window of the tent at the starlit sky, she thanked God for this opportunity and for letting her see people with needs that were far greater than her own. She thought of stories she'd heard about thirteen- and fourteen-year-old girls who went into prostitution. When Shelly was that age, she had worried about making the cheerleading squad in high school.

She learned of parents who wanted their children in school, but who could not afford it or who had no school available.

There was typhoid and tuberculosis. Many people died of starvation or disease in childhood or early adulthood.

Warm tears grew cool on Shelly's face. For the first time in months, she was crying for others. She was grateful to God for helping her see beyond herself and care about those so much less fortunate than she. She was glad that God could use her to reach out and help others. And if she needed proof that God worked in mysterious ways, she only had to look at how she had ended up in Haiti. God had worked through— *Trevor.*

eight

On the second Friday at supper the cooks surprised the group with a huge chocolate sheet cake. "Happy Birthday Shelly & Greg" was written in chocolate on the white icing. It was Shelly's twenty-second birthday and Greg's eighteenth. He was a young man from Louisiana who had just graduated from high school.

Another surprise was when Paul took Shelly aside to personally wish her a happy birthday and ask if he could take her into town Saturday evening to Le Perhoir Restaurant for dinner.

"I'd love it, Paul," she replied and wondered briefly if he had also asked Greg or if anyone else were going. She wasn't sure she should consider Paul's invitation as a date. Maybe he did this with everyone on the team who had a birthday, since none of them made any money and they weren't supposed to flaunt their wealth in front of the Haitians.

Early the next morning during breakfast the long, black car Shelly had seen at the airport drove up to the fence and Trevor got out. Little children rushed to him, pointing and chattering loudly. He stooped down, and the children touched his hair and picked at it. They laughed gleefully, and then he took packs of chewing gum from his pockets and distributed pieces to them. After coming inside the compound and speaking to Paul and some of the others, Trevor came over to Shelly.

As usual, the women had given Trevor the once-over. He did look rather nice in his light blue shirt and lightweight khaki pants. He had a light tan, and his eyes were sky blue in the early-morning freshness of a new day.

"Have you come to check up on our progress?" Shelly asked Trevor, glancing up at him. She'd thought little about him during the past two weeks, but it had been in the back of her mind that she expected him to check up on her.

"Nope," he said and handed her two cards, both of which were addressed to her in care of Trevor Steinbord at a Port-au-Prince general delivery address. While she opened them, he went over for a cup of coffee. The others moved to make room for him by Shelly when he returned.

The cards were from Shelly's parents and the Steinbords, and in each was a check. Shelly's laughter reflected her delight.

"This is like, 'Water, water, everywhere, and not a drop to drink'," she commented, holding up the checks. "How can I spend this?"

"Right over there is transportation," Trevor said, smiling as he gestured toward the black car that the Haitians were examining. "Paul assured me that you have the day off, so if you like, I can take you into town."

"Oh, Trevor. I really would like to get something new to wear tonight and maybe some lip gloss. I haven't worn any in over a month. Maybe I could even rent a room somewhere and take a real bath."

"Something. . .to wear tonight?" he asked carefully.

She looked at him with wide eyes. "Yes, Paul is taking me out to dinner at Le Perhoir. My birthday present."

"Paul?" he said slowly. "You mean Paul Sinclair?"

"Well, Paul Sinclair is the only Paul I know around here."

"Mmm. . ." He nodded and sipped his coffee. After a thoughtful moment he said, "Tell you what. I'll take you into town. There's someone I want you to meet. And maybe we can arrange for you to get your bath." He smiled. "Would it be all right for Paul to pick you up there?"

"That would be great, Trevor. Are we going to your place?"

"No," he said quickly. "We will go to Carmen's."

"Carmen?"

"That's who the car belongs to. She let me borrow it for this occasion."

"Occasion?"

"Yes, wishing you a happy birthday. And she suggested we meet at her place for lunch."

"She has a bathtub, huh?"

"Several," he replied, smiling.

As appealing as that was, Shelly wasn't sure about being around Trevor and some woman. She would probably feel even more uncomfortable and be forced to be civil to him. "Trevor, you don't have to go out of your way for me, you know. Just because we're both here in Haiti."

"No, and you don't have to accept, Shelly." He made a move as if to get up from the long wooden table.

"Wait!" She placed her hand on his forearm, then quickly moved it. "I accept. How can I turn down the possibility of a real bath?"

He laughed. "I'll tell Paul where to meet you this evening, while you get your things. And Shelly, what you're wearing will be just fine. The people here are accustomed to seeing tourists run around in casual clothes."

"If you say so," Shelly replied and was glad. Jeans were much more comfortable for shopping than a dress would be.

After packing a few items in her purse, she found Paul and Trevor talking.

"Did Trevor give you directions to wherever we will be?" she asked Paul.

"Yes," he said, with a warm expression in his dark eyes. "I'll be at Carmen's around six."

"Oooh, I'm looking forward to being a part of civilization again. But," she warned, mischievously, "you probably won't recognize the odor of cleanliness."

Paul laughed. "Enjoy your afternoon, Shelly," he called as she and Trevor turned to leave.

A sense of excitement pervaded Shelly as she settled in the car, turned toward Trevor, and drew her legs up onto the seat. "I feel like a bird out of a cage," she said.

"You'll be wanting to leave the project and have that vacation in Hawaii after all," Trevor said, glancing at her.

"No," she answered. "I wouldn't do that once I've made a commitment like this." She spread her fingers out on the legs of her jeans and grimaced at her hands. She wore the first calluses of her life. Her nails were trimmed short to prevent breakage. "Have you ever seen my nails in such pitiful condition?"

"You've always had lovely hands, Shelly."

Shelly's eyes flew to his, but he simply glanced out the window. She supposed a writer noticed little details like that. She looked at her hands again. "I like them better when they've been working hard than when they're just. . .looking pretty."

Their eyes met. Feeling a slight twinge of discomfort she said the first thing that popped into her mind. "Have you ever seen that weird man in the village who wraps his leg and foot around his neck and smokes cigarettes with his toes?"

Trevor laughed. "I did see him once. I suppose that's his claim to fame."

Wow, I'm doing great—Trevor has traveled the world, and I talk about a weird character who smokes with his toes! He must think I'm a real ninny!

She looked out the window as they neared a man walking along the side of the road, leading a donkey with bundles on its back. Two little boys skipped along beside them. The man and boys smiled and waved at the car.

Shelly tried to redeem herself from having spoken only of trite things. "I've always felt blessed and grateful, Trevor," she said. "But it's different when you're actually involved in the lives of people and see the needy face to face. I could never have understood unless I saw it for myself. I know we're helping these people. And. . .it's good for me in many ways." She was grateful he didn't push her to elaborate.

As Trevor drove up the winding road toward the villa, Shelly changed the subject. "Who is this. . .Carmen?" she asked.

"She translates my books into French," he explained. "Her husband is my publisher in France. I met them both about ten years ago when I first came to Haiti."

"That sounds fortunate."

"It was for me," he assured her. "Both were very helpful to a fledgling writer who knew little about the craft, and now they give me unlimited access to their guest house."

"Is her husband here too?"

"No, just Carmen. She takes an annual vacation away from everything and everyone in Paris—says it rejuvenates her."

He parked in the driveway, and they walked up onto the verandah. Spreading his hand out toward the landscape, Trevor half sang, "On a clear day—"

"You can see forever," Shelly interrupted, looking out.

"No. Just Port-au-Prince," he corrected, and they laughed together.

Suddenly she looked at him as he leaned against the ledge. He seemed different somehow. Always before, she'd thought of him as distant, morose, unapproachable. What had caused this new attitude?

Just then a woman came out to them.

Trevor introduced them, and Shelly was mildly surprised. When he spoke of Carmen as his translator, she had a mental picture of an older, intellectual type. But this woman, who looked to be in her early forties and was dressed in casual shorts and T-shirt, had the manner of a young woman. Her sandy, sun-streaked hair hung loosely below her ears and turned under slightly at the ends. She was not wearing makeup, but her face was naturally attractive.

"Oh, Shelly," Carmen exclaimed, holding out her hands. "Trevor told me what kind of ordeal they are putting you through this summer. A beautiful girl like you building a school. What can they be thinking of?"

Shelly liked Carmen immediately and took the extended hands. "But I volunteered, and it's good for me to work hard for a change. It makes me feel worthwhile."

"I manage to do that by translating Trevor's books and handling three teenagers in France for nine months out of the year." She raised thankful eyes toward heaven. "The summers are bliss when the three darlings go off to summer camps and then spend time here in Haiti where they monopolize my parents' time."

"You spend your summers here then?" Shelly asked.

"When the wars aren't going on," she said. "My husband will join me later. He can only take about a month off from his work. Sometimes we stay here, and sometimes we vacation in other places. So much depends upon his work schedule and our plans for the children."

"It sounds exciting," Shelly said. "And to think, I was all enthused about going into Port au Prince."

"Well, you have reason to be. But," Carmen added thoughtfully, "I think you'd like this shop in Petionville."

"Will they take a two-party check?" Shelly asked doubtfully.

"We'll stop by the Petionville Club. Antoine and I have been known there forever, so it's no problem. Of course, I could lend you money too, if it came to that." She turned to Trevor. "You are coming with us?"

"Well, somebody has to carry the packages and make sure nobody steals the car. I guess I'm elected."

For once, Shelly was glad Trevor would tag along. Carmen might know the area, but to her it was new and the mission leaders had warned against their roaming freely in the cities. She could imagine that people living in such poverty as she'd seen might do desperate things.

Carmen drove her black car, and Shelly sat in front. Trevor got in back.

"Oh, how beautiful!" Shelly exclaimed as they drove along the winding road to Petionville. "What is that red in those trees? I've never seen anything like it."

"The flamboyant," Carmen said. "It means 'flamelike' in French."

Trevor leaned forward. "They're also called 'poinciana'," he explained. "They grow as tall as oaks, and their crimson blossoms are the most beautiful during the month of June."

"Intermingled with them are the palms, juniper, breadfruit, and tamarind," Carmen added. "It's such a wonderful, un-spoiled setting."

"How did that French poet describe Petionville?" Trevor asked himself, and Shelly turned her head to see his face. "Oh, yes. He said it is a town at the foot of the mountains, with its head crowned with flowers, reminiscent of a lovely maiden who dreams of love by the side of the high road."

"That's lovely, Trevor," Carmen said, but Shelly felt the pain of it and knew that Trevor saw it in her eyes before she could look away. He grimaced as if the pain had struck him too. She was to have been married in June. She was like the mountain. Each June it would adorn itself and dream of love. Next June. . .and the next. . .and the next.

Giving herself a mental shake, Shelly dragged her thoughts back to the present. She had a responsibility as a guest, and her grief was no excuse for ignoring Carmen and Trevor.

As the car turned into the main square, Trevor pointed out different sites. "The Manoir des Lauriers," he said, "a show-place of the town." Then there was the Cabane Choucoune on the main square.

"If you were not going elsewhere tonight," Carmen said, "you might like to go there. It is the country's most famous night club. Port-au-Prince society goes there on Saturday nights."

"There's another place you'd like," Trevor said, and Shelly felt his voice very close to her ear. "Le Perchoir."

"Oh, yes," Carmen agreed enthusiastically. "In Boutilliers."

"The altitude is 3,000 feet and you can see—"

Shelly turned her head and saw that his face was very near hers. Wanting him to know she wasn't upset because of his repeating the poet's description, she allowed herself to give him a tiny smile. "You can see. . .Port-au-Prince?"

Trevor gazed into her eyes with a look Shelly couldn't identify. "No," he said. "Forever."

Paul arrived shortly before six, but Shelly wasn't quite ready. She'd spent too long in the luxurious bubble-bath. Her hair was still damp when she pulled it back from her face and fastened it in a thick bun at the back of her head. Nona had brought a collection of makeup and nail polish into the guest room so she could take her pick of anything she might need.

Shelly could hardly believe the woman in the mirror was the girl who did dirty, back-breaking labor every day. She didn't use any foundation since her face had tanned in spite of wearing a cap daily and her cheeks had a healthy glow. She applied a tad of green eye shadow, coral lip gloss, and a touch of powder on her nose and chin, and then brushed at her naturally arched eyebrows.

She stepped into the silk dress that felt cool and luxuriant against her freshly soaked skin that now smelled of perfumed lotion. The sleeveless top with a scooped neckline was fitted to the waist. The full skirt moved softly about her hips and fell to just above her knees. The soft coral material was covered with tiny clusters of flowers in pastel pink, orange, yellow, beige, and green. With its lapels of coral lace forming a V in front, a waist-length jacket of solid coral completed the outfit. Tiny pearl buttons trimmed in gold fastened down the front.

Carmen had been right. Her pearl drop-earrings hanging from a gold setting were perfect with the outfit. Shelly had bought beige sandals with two-inch high heels. She didn't want to appear taller than Paul, since he was only about two inches taller than she.

Hearing voices, she assumed Paul had arrived. Her nails weren't done yet, so she picked up a bottle of coral polish and went out to the verandah. Trevor was introducing Paul to Carmen, as Nona set a tray of glasses filled with lemonade on the wicker table.

After the introductions were completed, Paul, Trevor, and Carmen sat in wicker chairs near the table. Shelly asked them to excuse her so that she could polish her nails without exposing them to the odor. She took her glass and the polish over to the low wall that surrounded the verandah.

Paul looked quite handsome in a white short-sleeved shirt, tie, and dress pants. Looking down toward the parking area, Shelly saw a car that she assumed Paul had rented or borrowed.

Concentrating on her fingernails, Shelly wasn't quite sure how the conversation turned from Carmen's lovely villa, to Trevor's progress on his book, to Paul's report on the construction of the schoolhouse, to incidents occurring when she and Trevor were younger. Perhaps it was her birthday that triggered it. Anyway, Trevor was talking about being the one who told her when Don got the chicken pox.

"He told me I'd probably get them too, since the two of us always did everything together," Shelly said.

"Well, you'd just insulted me," Trevor returned.

Shelly gasped. "I? Insulted you? You're the one who called me a brat. That very day."

"I don't suppose you remember why?"

Shelly shrugged, painted another fingernail, and blew on it.

As if no one else were there, Trevor said, "I'd just showed you my new car, and what did you say?"

Her chin tilted. "I said it didn't look new, and I didn't like it."

"So I said I hoped you got the chicken pox because you deserved them."

"So I called you a smart aleck."

"See!" Trevor said, gesturing. "Could you blame me for calling her a brat? That was my first car. I'd just washed and waxed it, and along she comes to remind me it wasn't a new one."

"He always called me a brat," Shelly said defensively. "And I was just a sweet little girl."

Trevor grinned at Paul and Carmen. "What about the time you stuck your tongue out at me?"

"Oh, that was the year I thought I was so grown up. I went to my first formal dinner and wore a long dress and heels so high I waddled like a duck."

They all laughed at the description.

"Only one thing spoiled it," Trevor added. "And that was me. I drove Shelly and Don to the junior high prom and picked them up. I had just graduated from college and was about ready to leave for Haiti."

Shelly suddenly realized how much she and Trevor had been talking about themselves. Paul seemed to be enjoying it, but Carmen seemed quiet and thoughtful.

"I'm sure no one is interested in our childhood battles, Trevor."

"Oh, quite the contrary." Carmen spoke up quickly, a gleam in her eyes. "That summer was when I first met Trevor. He's a mystery everyone tries to unravel. So, how did he spoil that night?"

"Now it seems so silly," Shelly admitted. "But neither Don nor I would sit in front with Trevor. We climbed in back, and Trevor kept spying on us through the rearview mirror."

Trevor laughed out loud. "I did not."

"He did!" Shelly insisted. "I had thought I was so gorgeous, but after putting up with his spying, I simply had to stick my tongue out at him, and then I felt so infantile. What grown-up girl sticks her tongue out at a college graduate?

"I wasn't spying, Shelly," Trevor said in a serious tone. "I was looking. Because you *were* gorgeous."

She waited for him to say something else, to make those words sound like a joke, but silence filled the air. What happened to the gaiety? Trying to recapture it, she stammered, "Gorgeous. . .at fourteen?"

Trevor shrugged. "Fourteen, forty, seventy-four. . ."

"Anyway," she said, looking away from his silly expression, "I couldn't stand him."

She closed her mouth abruptly. What was happening? She'd said that as if it her objections to Trevor were in the past. But nothing had changed. She looked down and screwed the top on the polish, then blew at her nails again.

"Well, Paul," she said, looking over at him. "We'd better get to that restaurant before this *gorgeous* seventy-four-year-old looking creature shrivels up from starvation."

"That would take a lot of doing," Paul responded, standing.

Shelly gave him a coy look. "Are you intimating that I'm fat?"

"No," he said assuredly. "I'm saying it would take an awful lot for you to look anything but very beautiful."

"Carmen, what did you put in that lemonade?" Shelly jested, feeling a blush.

Carmen laughed, while Paul continued to look at her admiringly.

Suddenly it occurred to Shelly that she had not blanched with pain when they'd talked about her childhood and indirectly mentioned Don. Maybe time had helped her deal with her loss a little better.

❧

As Shelly and Paul walked down the steps, Trevor walked over to the ledge. He watched as Paul opened the car door for Shelly, then walked around to the driver's side. Paul looked up and gave Trevor a half-wave/half-salute in departing. Trevor nodded briefly in response. *Yes, I know you're a fine, Christian man, Paul. But I also know we all have our temptations and weaknesses.*

He watched the red tail lights until they disappeared around the final curve of the long winding road. He would liked to have warned Shelly. She was heart-broken; Paul was sensitive and caring and would respond to that. Paul had his own share of broken-heartedness. Shelly no longer sought only fun, and Paul was beyond that in personal relationships. It could be a dangerous time for each, yet a needful one. But he couldn't tell Shelly to be careful, as he had when she was a child. She was still a child in many ways, but how did one say that to a young woman celebrating her twenty-second birthday?

"That distant look, Trevor," Carmen said gently, coming to stand beside him.

He glanced around at her and smiled. Smiled, because he could give of himself to his work, to the world, get outside himself and his own selfish wants if it meant the good of another person. That had been a long, slow, painful process, and it continued.

"Thinking about your heroine?" Carmen asked carefully.

"Yes," he could say honestly, for he always thought about his heroine. Sometimes she was blond, sometimes she was a redhead, sometimes she was a dark beauty. She was short or tall, plump or trim, extroverted or introverted, down to earth or sophisticated, and yet she was the same—always the same. His heroine was always the unattainable, the unreachable, the untouchable, the one the hero could not, must not, would not, should not ever. . .

"Yes," he repeated to Carmen. "I was thinking about my heroine."

Carmen always said he was a mystery and she often looked at him questioningly. Tonight that question held a spark of knowledge, yet she said nothing, and she would say nothing, unless he allowed it.

She had known him when he was Shelly's age, lost, at loose ends, wondering what to do and where to turn—a young man trying to lose himself in work by day and in writing his feelings by night, then falling into an exhausted sleep.

He'd heard there was a publisher who vacationed in the villa on the hill, so, with nothing to lose, he'd gone there one day. Carmen saw his writing when it was rough and raw, filled with agony and confusion, but she saw something in it. She said he had a knack for fiction and called his work a novel even though she must have known it held his heart and soul.

It seemed unfair, somehow, to have become so successful from writing about things which he was simply trying to deal with—especially since those things continued to haunt him.

Trevor knew Carmen had invited Paul and Shelly to return for a late night *coffea arabica*. Shelly would need to come back and change her clothes anyway, since there was no place for luxuries at the work site.

Since there'd been little time for work that day, he and Carmen worked on the book. Carmen translated a chapter into French while he made changes she had suggested in another chapter.

Three hours had passed when they heard the car drive up. Shelly ran right in to change into her jeans and shirt, then joined them on the verandah where Nona set out the coffee. Shelly had let her hair down, and the balmy breeze teased it as she stood against the low wall in the light of the bright moon.

"Le Perhoir was much like this," she said, her eyes dancing like the stars in the sky and the lights far below in the city.

"All right," Paul said, "you practiced your French all the way here, now tell them what you ate."

"Certainly," she quipped. "Lobster."

"So far so good," Paul said, and they laughed.

She looked toward the sky. "*Rix aux. . .champions?*"

"Any takers?" Paul joked.

"*Champignons,*" Carmen said.

"Now, that's not the way you said it," Shelly accused.

"Well, she's from the real France. I'm only from Miami."

They all laughed and sipped their coffee.

"I hope you had their salad," Carmen said.

"Oh, yes," Paul replied.

"With *palmiste,*" Shelly put in.

"Touché," Carmen said, complimenting her accent.

Without finishing his coffee, Trevor stood. "I believe I'll turn in now," he said. There was an uncomfortable silence as he gathered a folder of papers, said good night, and headed for the steps.

"Could I give you a lift somewhere, Trevor?" Paul asked.

Trevor stopped and half-turned. "I'm only going out back to the guest house." He looked farther over his shoulder. "Happy birthday, Shelly."

"Thank you," she said, and for a moment, she thought he

looked. . .lonely.

"We'd better go too," Paul said. "There's an eleven o'clock curfew at the campsite."

Shelly took Carmen's hands in hers. "Thank you so much for your help today, Carmen. I really enjoyed being with you."

"You're welcome anytime," Carmen returned.

❧

Trevor saw the car lights and heard the car drive away. He stood in the shadow on his front porch and gazed into the darkness for a long time.

He remembered when he had returned to his brother's grave after the burial and tears of guilt had streaked his face and frozen in the November cold. He'd poured out his feelings to his brother and asked his forgiveness for the times the thought, *If only Shelly were not my brother's girl,* had crossed his mind. He'd made a promise to Don. He would try to help Shelly. Now, he renewed that vow—even if it meant helping her reach out to another man.

❧

During the rest of the summer, Shelly did not ask to return to Carmen's, nor did Trevor offer. He came to the campsite at least once a week, brought her mail, and talked with Paul and the other leaders. If she was near, he asked how things were going, but he made no special effort to seek her out.

Each Saturday she went out on the town, sometimes with friends, other times with a group that included Paul, and four times alone with Paul. On that first night Paul had spoken only of pleasant things, wanting to hear about North Carolina, telling her about the good things in his life in Miami and his past experiences in Haiti. It was the second time alone with him, at the beach, that he revealed his heartache.

He had been married and very much in love. He and his wife had a baby girl. One day, when the child was two years old, they had put her down for a nap. He and his wife had decided to go to bed also. His wife got up first and went to the nursery. She yelled his name. Paul ran. The baby wasn't there.

"Didn't you put the gate up?" she asked.

"No, I thought you would," he said as they called and searched the house. Then, following his most horrible instinct, he went to the glass door leading to the patio. It was partially open. He saw the baby face down in the pool. He ran, jumped into the pool, and got the baby out while his wife stood screaming.

"Call 911," he commanded between breaths of trying to revive the baby. He couldn't.

"She blamed me. I blamed her. We blamed ourselves," Paul said, pouring out his torture while he and Shelly cried. "We relived that scene every waking and sleeping moment. Why didn't both of us check to make sure the gate was across the doorway? Why hadn't we checked to make sure the patio door was locked? How could we have been enjoying our love for each other while our baby was struggling to live—and died?"

He'd turned his tear-stained face to Shelly. "We were never able to enjoy each other again. We forgave. We understood. We learned. We grew. And we grew apart. We could not forget. Can never forget." He paused. "She's remarried now. Has two children."

And it was because of his honesty that Shelly could pour out her own tortured feelings to Paul. He understood. He needed to talk of his experience, although it had happened ten years earlier. He knew she needed to talk too. She felt as if she were growing, just as the school building was growing day by day. A work was being completed. Something good was being finished.

Finally, in mid-August, it was done: a fine two-story building. It was dedicated. That Saturday, the entire crew celebrated at the beach. Shelly and Paul walked far down the sandy shore, away from the others.

"My summers here in Haiti are a giving of myself that brings a satisfaction that no paid job could do," Paul told her. "I watch Christians grow. Many of them are strongly committed and the summer strengthens them for their inevitable times of trouble. Others, like you, come for various reasons and find something—even if it is only a constructive passing of time. And it is constructive—now there stands a school building where children can learn and grow, develop their minds and spirits. It's good. Very good."

"Paul, I can't begin to tell you what it's meant to me, personally. I needed someone to talk to and it couldn't have been just anyone."

He stopped and took her hands in his. "You've taught me much this summer."

"Me?" she questioned, feeling it was the other way around.

Paul nodded. "Yes. You've made me realize that I do need a woman in my life. I had forced myself to believe that I didn't."

Shelly tried to move her hands away from his, but his grip tightened. His smile was warm. "Don't look so desolate. I'm not proposing. Not that I wouldn't like to. You're more than I could even hope for. But I know I'm not the man for you. I've known that all along."

"Oh, Paul, you're one of the finest men I know. And you've become a dear, dear friend. And besides that," she said honestly. "I really love you in a way."

He spoke seriously. "We've developed a beautiful thing, a fine friendship. If we let it, maybe it could grow to be more. I could take you into my life without a moment's hesitation, except I know I'm not the great love of your life."

"No one is."

He smiled. "Life isn't over for you. It's just beginning. You need a chance to find out what is out in the world before you give up on it."

She hoped he might be right.

He let go of her hands, and they began walking back toward the others. "Thanks, Shelly. Your caring has been a turning point in my life. You've helped me open up my heart for commitment."

She wondered if that would ever be true for her.

ᕚ

On the night before team members were to leave Haiti, Trevor joined Paul, Pastor and Mrs. Zabute, and the Haitian school officials at their table during supper. After all the speeches of gratitude were made and they were dismissed, Trevor approached Shelly.

"I'd like to talk to you before I leave. But first, I have some business to conduct."

"Sure, send someone to my tent."

Later, as the sky was turning mauve, she met Trevor in the dining area and they walked outside. Several others stood around watching the sun set.

"What's your verdict, Shelly?" Trevor asked as they headed toward the water. "Are you glad you came to Haiti?"

"It's a side of life I'm glad I didn't miss," she replied, stopping to study the view. "I've discovered there's more to me than cheerleading, as satisfying as it was at the time. Football games and pizzas were an important part of my life. Going to church on Sunday in a pretty dress and a smile on my face was important. But honestly, I felt more beautiful nailing those boards together than dressing up for a party."

"There is room for both," Trevor said, and they strolled along a path and sat on a bench beneath a palm tree.

"Yes. I'm glad I came, Trevor. At first, I did it because you presented it to me and there was nothing worth doing that mattered anyway. Then I began doing it because of the need around me. I didn't do it for any kind of reward, but I have been rewarded more than anyone."

"You're growing up," he said.

For once, she didn't resent his words. "I thought I was grown up."

He smiled. "We all do from about age thirteen to thirty. Then we begin to learn."

She laughed lightly. Trevor seemed so different than she had always thought him to be. Sometimes she had to remind herself that she didn't like him. Her dislike of Trevor seemed to be more like a memory than a reality.

"I'm on my way back to Hawaii," he said, "Sure you won't join me?"

"Maybe I should," she said, to his surprise. Then she added, "Or I could take Paul up on a vacation in Florida. But I realize I've got to stop drowning in my sorrow and find some permanent way to reach out to others. It's the only way, isn't it?"

"Yes," he said, and seeing that Paul was beginning to encourage team members to head toward their tents since it would soon be dark, Trevor stood. "Give the families my love, Shelly."

Trevor did not watch her walk toward Paul. Instead, he stood like a stone, watching the sun sink into the horizon and the world turn gray.

nine

On the flight back to North Carolina, Shelly had several hours in which to think about her future. She could use a vacation and Hawaii was appealing, but it would be too stressful coping with Trevor in his own territory. And, in a way, she felt her entire life had been one big vacation up until Don died. Now, after a summer of hard work and giving of herself to help others, she felt she needed to get right into involving herself with other people.

As soon as she arrived home, the decision was made for her.

"We didn't want to tell you while you were in Haiti, Shelly," her mother said when she met her at the airport, "but your father had a little problem. It's his heart."

Fear struck deep in Shelly's heart. Since the tragedy that took Don's life, she imagined the worst kind of scenario. She could not relax in the car on the way to the hospital nor tell about her own summer. Not until she saw her father.

He was sitting up in his hospital bed, reading *Time* magazine, when she rushed to his side. How strange to see him in a bed instead of beside it, bringing treatment and comfort to others.

"It was a mild heart attack," her dad said, "caused by cholesterol buildup back in the days when I didn't know better than to drink whole milk." He patted Shelly's hand reassuringly. "I'll be better than ever as soon as they let me get out of here."

"Sure you will, Daddy." Shelly was grateful for his positive attitude but feared he would never be the robust, seemingly-invincible man he'd always been.

Instead of Shelly, it was her mom and dad who took a

month's vacation once her father was discharged from the hospital. Margo and Hanlan told them Trevor would remain in Haiti for several more weeks and had offered them his house in Hawaii. Of course, Shelly was included in the invitation.

"Sure you won't change your mind and go with us?" her mother asked for the umpteenth time.

"Not unless you need me, Mom," she replied.

Shelly wanted to be alone and knew her parents also needed time for themselves. She was beginning to look at her parents and life in a different way. It was time for her to become independent and think about providing for her own future.

But the cares of others were bent on following Shelly. In early October just after her parents returned from Hawaii, Gran had a light stroke. The only damage was a slight paralysis on the left side of her body and face, and the doctors said there was every reason to be optimistic. The Steinbords insisted that Gran stay with them, so Shelly helped with her during the day and taught a few exercise classes at night at Gran's health club.

Gran's speech was affected, but Shelly could understand her perfectly well. "When I go, Shelly, I'll tell Don that you're doing fine. He will be glad to hear that." Shelly could only nod and they both would cry.

But it was Trevor Gran spoke of most often. He was her first grandson and held a special place in her heart. "Have you read his books?" Gran asked one afternoon.

"No, I've never taken the time."

"You should."

"Are they. . .really good?"

Gran got a far-away look. "They make me proud—and sad."

Shelly didn't question in what way. She could understand that Gran would be proud of Trevor's success. But Shelly didn't need to feel proud of Trevor, and she certainly didn't want to feel sad.

November began with the encouraging news that her dad could return to work at the hospital on a limited basis. Then Gran had another stroke. She died three days before the anniversary of Don's death.

"Do not mourn for me. I'm going to a better place," Gran had said many times, and she had planned every detail of her passing. Her body was donated for research, and the family held a private memorial service in accordance with her instructions.

Shelly was not surprised that Gran had left her some choice pieces of jewelry. But she was surprised at what else she left her. Gran had left her businesses to her grandchildren and Shelly. In a letter she had left to have read after her death, Gran wrote, "Shelly is like my own granddaughter. And since she was so close to Don, I want her to have his share." Katrina and Betsy would have control of the boutique. Trevor and Shelly would have joint ownership of the health club.

Trevor had come home to be with his family as soon as he heard of Gran's death. His family and Shelly's went to the Grove Park Inn for dinner and to discuss the business arrangements.

"Here I was, all prepared to get into something where I could be useful to people," Shelly said. "Now, this! I know we're all like one big family. . .almost. But," she continued, "I think I should give it all to. . .to Trevor. I really shouldn't have. . .half of that business."

"Don't you think you can handle it?" Trevor asked.

Her eyes flashed. "I cut my teeth on that health club. Don and I were there almost every day. That's why Gran wanted to leave it to him. She knew what it meant to him. And you weren't around to know it, but I've filled in many days for every class that's taught there, from nutrition to aerobic exercise."

"Then why do you want to throw it all away?"

"I don't," she protested, looking around for some encouragement, but the rest of the family was eating, as if the conversation wasn't occurring. Things always were strange when Trevor was around! "I'm giving it to you!"

"I'm not taking it," he said calmly.

"It. . .it doesn't mean anything to you?"

"I live in Hawaii, remember? So, since you're giving it all to me, I'll just sell it and pocket the money."

"You can't be serious!"

He shrugged. "What else can I do? I can't be here to run it. Would you like to manage it? I'll pay good wages."

"This is unbelievable!" she muttered, looking up toward the overhang of the porch where they were dining. "Why would I work for you at a manager's salary when I could be co-owner?"

He shrugged. "I don't know. You're the one who doesn't want to keep it in the family."

"That's absurd. It's just that I don't think I deserve it."

"You think I do?"

She hesitated. "It doesn't matter. You're. . .family."

"Gran apparently thought of you as family," he returned.

"Yes, but I don't want to be selfish."

"Fine. Then I'll take it. Sell it. And go home to Hawaii."

"That is not what Gran wanted!"

"What did she want?"

"She wanted to keep it in the family."

"Then I see only one way for that to happen," he said.

Shelly took a deep breath, waiting.

Finally, he continued. "I don't intend to have any part in running the health club. So it's up to you. You can give it to me, although I can't imagine why you would want to give me such an expensive gift—"

"Because you're so pleasant," she said with undertones of sarcasm.

"He's always been sweet," Betsy agreed, and the sisters laughed.

He grinned at his sisters, then addressed Shelly again. "If you don't want it, then I have no choice but to sell it. I have my career, and it doesn't include operating a health club. Now, if you think you can make a go of it—proceed."

"You think I can't," she said.

His eyebrows lifted. "It might be a little tougher than building a school. As I remember, you struggled with math in high school. There will be books to keep. . ."

While she fumed, he smiled. "Tell you what. I accept your gift," he said.

Shelly felt downcast. Gran had given her a beautiful gift, and she had let it slip through her fingers—and it would no longer be in the family.

"But I accept it only if you agree to certain conditions," he added, and she looked at him quickly. "You run the health club for a year, and if it's worthwhile and profitable, then we'll talk about what to do."

"I'm not working for you," she said.

"Then I guess you'd better stay on as co-owner. You can pay yourself whatever salary you like if you manage the place or work in it. But don't expect me to have any part of it."

"I suppose that's fair enough," she said, rising to the challenge. "If I can't run it successfully by the end of a year, then I don't deserve it, and I suppose it's your right to do whatever you want with it."

"Deal," he said and thrust out his hand across the table toward her.

Shake hands on a business deal with Trevor Steinbord? The families were looking now. "What. . .what do you all think?" She hoped he would withdraw his hand.

They all shook their heads as if they had no idea. "That's between the two of you," Hanlan said and then turned to start a conversation with her father.

Shelly reluctantly stuck out her hand, and Trevor enclosed it in a strong but gentle grasp. It couldn't have lasted more than a few seconds, but somehow it seemed longer. Maybe it was because he said the most unexpected thing. "And Shelly, if you need or want my help, just let me know." Then he gave a smile that reached his eyes, and for an instant she couldn't look away.

Self-consciously, she returned her hand to her lap and thought it trembled slightly when she touched it with her other hand. Well, no wonder! She'd just committed herself to a year of proving something to Trevor Steinbord.

꿈

Shelly and her parents spent a lot of time with the Steinbords during Christmas. They'd gone through a Christmas without Don, and now they'd go through it without Gran as well. For the first time in years, Trevor didn't come home. He had to fly to France for a consultation with his publisher.

Then good news came. Peggy and John were getting married in January, and Peggy wanted Shelly to be a bridesmaid. Having heard many times that the Steinbords were like her second family, Peggy had invited them to attend as well. It gave them all something to look forward to.

The week before the wedding, Shelly flew to Peggy's home. The Landons and the Steinbords travelled together, arriving later in the week. The wedding was beautiful.

Shelly cried.

But that was acceptable at weddings.

꿈

As Shelly became more involved in the workings of the health club, she became more determined to show Trevor Steinbord that she could run the business without his help. However, it was rough going. Each time she had a new idea, Ted pooh-poohed it and she backed down, believing he knew the business since he'd been manager for eight years. She knew how to teach aerobics, so she did, while slowly trying to learn what all went on behind the scenes. The older clientele dropped off considerably after Gran's death, and Shelly knew they must have been friends of Gran.

"We're going in the hole," Ted said in February.

"Let me see the books," she said. "Maybe I can figure something out."

Trevor had been right when he intimated that she was not a math whiz. However, she did know when outgo exceeded income, and rather than fire any of the employees, Shelly went without salary for a couple of months.

"Maybe it'll pick up in the spring," Ted said.

But it didn't, and Ted had no ideas about what to do and even intimated it was her fault since everything had been going great before she took over. Then when the club reached the brink of bankruptcy, Ted asked for a raise. He said he had a good offer from another club and he'd have to consider it since his wife just had another baby.

"Then take it!" Shelly snapped, fed up and disappointed in Ted, and in herself. She knew her family or the Steinbords would help out, and of course she could contact her *silent partner*—but only as a last resort.

Then finally, she prayed. *Lord, if this is not right, then it should fail. If You have something else in mind for me, let me know. In the meantime, all I know to do is continue and ask that You shut doors I shouldn't go through. I will try to do this for You and for others, and not just to prove something to myself and Trevor Steinbord.*

Shelly decided it wouldn't hurt to try some of the ideas she'd had at the beginning. She could save money by not hiring a manager, but she had to have a bookkeeper, so she advertised for one.

"Hi," sounded a male voice several days later when she was at her desk pouring over invoices. She looked up. "Jake? Jake Simmons! Where'd you come from?"

She and Don had gone to high school with Jake. He was a year older and hadn't participated in sports, so he wasn't in their crowd. But she'd known him for years since they'd attended the same church. She hadn't seen him in a long time.

Jake slouched against the doorframe and pushed at his wire-framed glasses. "I, um, saw the ad in the paper. I thought this was the place run by the Steinbords, but I didn't know that you. . .you know. . ."

She realized that Jake was nervous. Did he come about the ad? "Sit down, Jake, and tell me what you've been doing," she said, hoping to put him at ease.

He sat in the leather chair across from her. She'd never noticed him in particular, but she now had the impression that he'd lost weight. But he had the same straight light brown hair, no receding hairline, and his gray eyes looked sad. "I was sorry to hear," his voice lowered, "about Don."

"Thanks," she said and clicked a ball-point pen unconsciously.

"Are you working here. . .or something?" he asked. "I mean, you're sitting behind the desk."

Shelly smiled wryly. "I'm trying to make a go of this place, Jake, and not doing a very good job." She didn't want to drop her troubles on him. "The worst part is the bookkeeping. I've advertised. . ."

"Yeah, I know," he said. "That's why I'm here."

"What?"

"Well, like I say, I saw the ad."

"You're a bookkeeper?"

"My mom kept the books for Dad's hardware store, and she showed me a lot. I got interested and went on to Western Carolina and majored in accounting. I'm working for my dad now. My mom had a bout with cancer, you know. She's in remission now, but Dad says she's to stay home and take it easy. But I need something else to tide me over, so when I saw the ad, I thought. . ."

"Your dad probably pays more than I could, Jake."

"No, I'm looking for something in addition to that. Maybe evenings or even weekends."

"That would take a lot of your time."

"Time's all I've got right now," he said, and she saw the muscles tighten in his jaw. "I guess I need to be totally honest with you, Shelly."

Jake talked about his marriage to Mandy right out of high school. He was working for his dad, and Mandy worked at McDonald's. They had a cute apartment. But after Mandy got pregnant, she also got too sick to work and finally had to quit. The debts piled up, but they thought having a baby would make the problems disappear. Then after their little girl was born, it got worse. They'd never have believed a baby took so much time and money. Buying diapers alone could send a family to the poor house. Mandy's and Jake's parents helped the best they could, but then Jake's mother got sick. Mandy complained all the time, and Jake started running around with his old buddies and drinking.

"I'm to blame," Jake admitted. "Mandy moved back in with her parents, and they gave my little girl everything. I tried to get Mandy back, but she said she married too young and isn't ready to settle down. She got a divorce and custody of little Jenny. Her parents could take care of the baby and mine couldn't—with mom sick and all. I didn't contest the divorce, and I was in no shape to take care of my little girl. So now Mandy's going back to school, and her mom is taking care of the baby—she's three now." Jake choked on the words, "I have to pay child support and. . .I can see her every weekend."

"I'm sorry," Shelly said tearfully, sensing how deeply Jake was hurting. "I have to ask this, Jake. Do you have a drinking problem now?"

"I honestly don't think so. It was an escape for me, but it ended up making things worse and proving I couldn't handle my life properly. I guess I proved my immaturity. I don't want that kind of life. I'm getting back into church now. They have a singles' group that's real supportive."

Shelly looked into his hurting eyes and told him how little she could pay.

"I'll take it," he said.

As it turned out, Jake caught several mistakes that Ted had made in the bookkeeping. The health club wasn't as bad off as it had appeared. Ted had also raised the prices on patrons twice in the past year. "That's not good business," Jake said. "Here's what I would suggest."

So, with Jake's suggestions and Shelly's innovative ideas, by summer the health club was on the up-swing. Shelly scheduled classes for all ages in various levels of aerobics, weight lifting, swimming, folk dance, and nutrition. So many signed up, she hired another instructor for the summer, a Phys. Ed. teacher from the local university.

By November, the business appeared solvent—even better off than when Gran had owned it and Ted managed it. Not only did they still have loyal clients from Gran's day, but new clientele were being added every day. Parents had been enthusiastic about the summer program and were looking forward to next year's, and the club had enough new members to get it through the winter slump.

&a

Although there was a light snow in October, the first really cold spell hit in November. The mountain roads were icy. Shelly could feel depression coming on and tried to fight it by spending more evenings at the club and lining up next summer's classes. It was good having Jake there in the evenings, either working or pumping iron, and she marveled at how his self-esteem had improved, as well as his physique.

Again, she realized the value of staying busy and reaching out to others, rather than wallowing in self-pity. That was easier said than done, however, as the one year anniversary of Gran's death came and went and the date of Don's death loomed closer. She sent a donation to the college scholarship fund in his memory.

The second anniversary of his death came on a Saturday, one of the club's busiest days. After closing at 11:00 P.M., Shelly and Jake stayed. Shelly was still in her leotard, picking up stray towels and putting equipment back in its place. Jake was working out on the weight bench. It was a difficult weekend for him because his little girl was sick and he wouldn't see her again for a week. "She doesn't need me," Jake said fearfully, sitting up. "Mandy's seeing somebody now, and he's going to take my place."

He grabbed his towel, wiped his hands and his face, then threw the towel down. "I'd better get out of here before I blubber like a baby."

Shelly went over to him and touched his arm. "Jake, it's okay. I've been holding back all day, and I'm waiting for the clock to strike midnight. Two years ago today, Don. . ."

"Oh, Shelly. I'm sorry," he said and turned.

They held each other tightly for a long moment.

"Excuse me," a stern voice said at the same time a rap sounded on the door.

Startled, Shelly's head jerked toward the sound.

Standing in the doorway, like a bull about to paw the dirt, was none other than Trevor Steinbord.

Even the icy blue accusation in his eyes could not cool the heat Shelly felt rushing along her skin.

"How did you. . ." Shelly began as he held up a key. Of course, he'd have a key. He was the owner. "I. . .we. . .never mind," she said, letting go of Jake's arms.

"Mr. Steinbord," Jake mumbled, with a guilty look on his face. He picked up his towel and wiped his arms and chest as if he were wiping away the embrace. Then he found his shirt and put it on.

"Do we know each other?" Trevor asked.

"You probably don't know me, but everybody around here knows you," Jake said, as if Trevor were someone special. After Shelly introduced him as the bookkeeper, he offered to show Trevor the books.

"Another time," Trevor said, "I was just passing by and saw the cars parked outside and no front lights on so I thought I'd better stop in and see if everything was all right." He went over and sat on a stool behind the reception desk as if he planned to stay.

"Look, I'll go on home if that's okay, Shelly," Jake said.

"Sure, and thanks for staying," Shelly said. "I guess I'll see you at church in the morning."

Jake nodded. He and Trevor said good night.

"Just happened to be passing by, huh?" Shelly said skeptically, reaching over to take her sweat pants from a rack, step into them, and pull them over her leotard.

He nodded as she slipped her arms into the sweat jacket and zipped it up. "Been up to Chestnut Lodge to see Elliot."

Shelly went over to the desk. "You mean Elliot Maxwell?"

"Yep. He's tying the knot next month."

"With Meera Briskin. The whole town's talking about it."

"I'm sure it is," Trevor agreed with a laugh. "Their families have been feuding longer than the Hatfields and McCoys. Then these two fall in love and prove that love can overcome any obstacle. Miracles do happen."

Shelly smiled, thinking about it. "Meera has come in here a couple times, but I was surprised to get an invitation to the wedding."

Trevor didn't appear surprised. "It's going to be a huge wedding. They're inviting friends of friends." He smiled. "Elliot and I have been friends since grade school days. He and Josh Logan and I," he said reminiscently.

"You're in the wedding?"

"A groomsman," he said. "Josh will sing."

"Josh is a member. Have you been working behind the scenes?" she asked, with a growing suspicion.

"Well, I do have a stake in this, you know."

Shelly looked toward the ceiling. "And I thought I drummed

up the business."

"Without you," he said pointedly, "there wouldn't be a business."

"Are you ready to take it over?" she asked, trying not to care.

"Do you want to give it up?" he asked.

"I've. . .put a lot of time and effort into it."

He looked at her a long time. "Is it successful?"

"We've begun to make a profit. I've bought some new equipment."

"I noticed that," he said, glancing toward the weight benches.

"And with the advice of your dad's financial advisor, I've invested a little."

He raised his eyebrows. "What about your salary?"

"Oh, I'm paying myself manager wages." She laughed lightly. "But no bonuses or paid vacations."

"Didn't your partner tell you?" he asked, as if serious. "You've earned a month's paid vacation."

"Partner" was the word that registered with Shelly. But since they'd shaken hands on the deal they had made in front of his family and hers, he could claim the health club as his own at any time. "I suppose you want a report of our progress?"

"Not now," he said, getting off the stool. "We should go. It's past midnight."

She gave him a quick look. He smiled, went over to the light switch, and waited until she got her keys. Then he held the door open for her to walk out into the crisp November night.

☙

Trevor was delighted that his friend Elliott had won the love of Meera Briskin and that their feuding families had made peace with each other. Standing with the other groomsmen at the front of the church, he looked at Josh, whose mane of curly hair and heavy long beard were vividly orange-red above his black tux. He was spotlighted as he sang in his rich baritone voice "The Twelfth of Never."

Trevor's eyes moved to Elliot and Meera as the throbbing

sounds permeated the church: "Until the twelfth of never, I'll still be loving you." He saw the look of love and expectancy in their eyes. Elliot was his own age. He remembered back when Elliot and Josh's sister Kate had been dating. Then Kate had been killed. As the years passed, Elliot had wondered if Kate had been the only girl for him and if there would never be another. Now, after almost ten years, he was in love, vowing to give his life and love to his beautiful bride, who less than a year ago had been his family's enemy. *The near-impossible could happen!*

And Josh, in his early thirties, still single, often confided that God might want him to remain single. But he didn't want to. *And neither do I, Josh. It's not easy, friend. I know.* But Josh was as happy as Trevor that Elliot had found his love. After their vows were spoken, the couple knelt at the altar while Josh sang "The Lord's Prayer."

The reception was held in the lobby at Chestnut Lodge, which was owned by Elliot's parents. After many introductions and renewing acquaintances, Trevor had a chance to walk off alone and look out a window. A light snow had begun to fall. City lights glimmered like Christmas lights far below in the valley.

"Come on, buddy," came the baritone voice of Josh, as he grasped Trevor's arm. "Let's see if you can catch the garter."

Trevor scoffed. "I have no use for a woman's garter."

"You have a better chance now than ever," Josh said pointedly, and Trevor knew his friend alluded to the fact that he and Shelly owned a business together.

Trevor smiled at his cup of punch, then set it on a table and followed Josh over to the right of the staircase where other bachelors had gathered. Guests were looking up. Following their gaze, Trevor saw Meera and Elliot standing on the second level. She leaned over slightly and tossed her bouquet from the left side of the staircase.

Trevor watched as the bouquet fell toward the single

women. Shelly stood near the group, laughing, but she didn't reach for the bouquet. It fell into the grasping hands of Louisa, Meera's cousin and maid of honor.

Then Elliot threw the garter. The tall, burly Josh had no problem reaching higher, quicker than the others and catching it. Glancing to his left, Trevor saw that Shelly was watching with a question in her eyes. Was she wondering why he hadn't reached for the garter? Did she still wonder why he had never married? Trevor sighed. How many years would slip by before Shelly realized what he felt for her?

❧

Three days later, Trevor went to the health club, and Shelly gave him a complete accounting of everything that had been done in the past year. By the time she'd finished, he understood even better than when his mom and sisters had written their accounts just how hard she'd worked, how much she'd put into it. He would be glad to say, "It's yours, Shelly. All yours," but he didn't want to let go of this one contact with her.

It was she who asked, "What do you want me to do now?"

"Let's just keep things as they are for awhile. By the way, the family is going to a candlelight service on Christmas Eve. Would you like to join us?"

"The Singles are having a children's Christmas party in the afternoon. After that, Jake and I are taking his little girl to see a live nativity scene and then to look at Christmas lights."

"His. . .little girl?"

She nodded. "His wife divorced him and now she's seeing someone else. He only gets to see his little girl on weekends." She spoke with compassion. "It's real hard for Jake being single again. He has his shyness to overcome, as well as his feeling of being a failure."

Trevor tried to sound understanding as his world crashed in on him.

Later that snowy night, as Trevor and Josh rode around the

mountains in Josh's Jeep, Trevor spoke of the irony of it. "No one seems to suspect we're not completely satisfied, Josh. After all, we both are set in our chosen careers."

Josh shook his heavy mane of red hair, and his thick beard moved as his big smile transformed his face. "We've learned the hard way, Trev—stay busy and reach out to the world."

Then Josh, the psychology teacher/counselor/singer did the unexpected. He rolled down his window, causing Trevor to hug his own jacketed arms to himself. Josh's melodious tones echoed across the otherwise silent valley, which was blanketed in snow. *"Let it snow, let it snow, let it snow. . ."*

❧

Returning to Hawaii after Christmas, Trevor had to go through the same painful process he'd gone through numerous times before—giving his emotional life over to God. It seemed he always took it back, allowing hope to spring forth in his heart and mind, and he was helpless to rid himself of her memory.

"Here she is again, Lord," he prayed, looking up at the starlit sky as he walked along his private beach. The sound of the waves caressing the shore interrupted his musings. It was as if the water was trying to grab the sand and take it with it. But sand was illusive, and the water seemed to groan as it receded from the beach, helpless, empty. Then it tried again. . . and again. . .and again.

"Like me, Lord," Trevor whispered. His voice seemed to shiver on the breeze, as the water trembled on the shore and spread out aimlessly.

He knew himself well enough to know he'd never give up hope that Shelly might someday love him unless someday she was happily married to someone else. Even then, he would always retain her memory.

"Help me to want what's best for her, Lord," he prayed, as he had a thousand times. "You know how much I want her. I believe she's right for me. But if I'm not right for her, and it seems that I must not be, then help me either to become the kind of person she can love or to accept that the answer to my heart's desires is 'no.' I'm giving this emotional quandary to You again, Lord. I know I keep taking it back, almost as often as the waves keep trying to take the beach back into the ocean with them. The beach remains, Lord. The water recedes. That's how it must be. Help me to accept what must be."

ten

One evening, right after the new year, Shelly had just finished teaching her 8:00 P.M. aerobics class and was sitting at her desk giving serious thought to an international aerobics contest brochure, when the receptionist buzzed her phone.

"Shelly, there's someone here to see you. He wouldn't say who he is, but he says he knows you. He's headed for your office."

Shelly looked up and saw him walking toward her open door. It was like seeing a ghost from another lifetime. She caught her breath. "Ben? Ben Martin?" she said, half rising from the chair while holding onto the desk.

"None else!" In his quick laugh, she caught a glimpse of the old Ben Martin she'd known in college, an agile receiver on the football team who kept others laughing with his jokes and quick wit. Now, he stood like a shadow of himself. His body was thin. "You'd better sit down," he said, then added with an attempt at humor, "and so had I."

Then she realized he was holding onto the door casing, and when he stepped inside the room, his body seemed to lean forward in a slightly unnatural way. She doubted she would have noticed had he not made his last comment and if she hadn't heard he'd been badly hurt the night of the tragic accident.

Ben lowered himself into the chair that Shelly indicated opposite her on the other side of the desk. "I've been thinking about coming in since last year when I read about your summer program and that you were the new manager."

"I should have been the one, Ben—"

He waved away her remark. "I had to be ready for this, Shelly. I haven't found it easy to face people."

"You seem to be doing okay now," she said softly.

He lowered his head, then lifted his gaze to hers. "My therapist said I have to do this." Then he grinned.

She grinned too and remembered a long time ago Trevor had said something about crawling and learning to walk again. She wondered where she was on that journey.

"I haven't kept in touch with Nell—or anyone," Shelly admitted.

"Whew," said Ben. "That was the toughest part." Pain settled in his eyes. "I thought I was doing okay and could accept the loss of my leg. But Nell took one look at the hospital covers lying against the bed where my leg should have been. She just stood there staring and screaming. It cut deep."

"I'm sorry," was all Shelly knew to say.

He nodded. "It's okay now. I think it was harder on her than on me. But at the time it seemed like all our feelings for each other were in that leg. She couldn't seem to see the rest of me. That set me back for awhile." His grim look left his face as he reached into his pocket and drew out a wallet. "My new life," he said with a smile. The picture was of a smiling woman about Shelly's age with her arm around the shoulders of a small boy dressed in a baseball uniform.

For the next hour they talked about the changes they'd made in their lives during the past two years. Ben had a job in a sporting goods store in a mall. The woman worked next door in a dress shop. She was a single parent who'd had a rough time raising her child. She and Ben were dating.

"I'm even going to help coach Little League this spring," he said proudly. "Little guys seem to think my prosthesis is real neat."

Shelly felt good about his visit. "Come work out with us sometime," she invited.

"Hey, that might be a way of moonlighting if you'd let me charge admission." He laughed after he said it, but Shelly realized the seriousness of it. Although he was obviously glad to have a prosthesis, he was self-conscious about it.

After he left, Shelly couldn't get Ben out of her mind. He came to represent an entire group of people she hadn't wanted to think about: the football players who had lived and the loved ones of those who hadn't.

"I'm ashamed of myself," Shelly said to her parents the next morning, after telling them of Ben's visit. "I've been too wrapped up in the business and in practicing for an aerobics contest to contact any of them."

"Hold on now, Kitten," her dad was quick to say. "There's nothing wrong with your trying to excel in your profession. And besides, you've been going through the process of healing too. Take it from a doctor: there's a lot more to healing than just physical recovery. Sometimes that's the easiest thing to fix."

"Well, now that I'm thinking of other people, it's time I did something," Shelly said pointedly. "I'd like to open up the health club one night a week to the disabled. Free of charge."

Her mother came over and hugged her. "I'm so proud of you, darling."

"So am I," her dad said, "but I don't think they'd like the idea of charity. You should charge at least a nominal fee."

After that, Shelly talked with anyone she thought might give her some sound advice on her ideas, including her parents, Jake, the Steinbords, and even Josh when he came into the health club.

"Maybe you can give me some advice," she began, "since you're a counselor."

"I'll do my best, Shelly," he said with a big smile, while patting his stomach. "I might even decide to work on this physique of mine."

Two weeks later, definite plans were underway. Josh had contacted a local representative for the Handicapped Adults Program, and he was excited about the possibilities. The following week, Shelly met with Josh, the representative, two other officials of HAP, and three physical therapists from the hospital who had volunteered when her father made the need known. By the end of the meeting it was decided that Thursday evenings would be set aside for the handicapped. Men and women would meet at 7:00 P.M. for an inspirational or informational time. Then they would be separated according to their particular needs and capabilities.

An entire spread in Sunday's paper resulted in constant phone calls for the rest of the week. The college was most cooperative about helping to secure information on the whereabouts of the football players injured two years before.

When Shelly mentioned to Margo and Hanlan Steinbord that she planned to contact the injured football players and the friends and family of those who had died, they offered their home for a meeting place. "We would love to have a part in this, Shelly," they said.

Shelly took them up on it since their house was bigger than the Landons' and more functional in any kind of weather. The entire lower floor was equipped for informal entertaining, and they had a huge outdoor pool and patio area.

At Josh's suggestion, Shelly made up a schedule of tentative activities, and he even agreed to come for the sharing sessions since Shelly felt someone with training and experience should conduct them. By April, Shelly was getting favorable responses from the people she'd contacted. All but two could come, and the two would couldn't make it thought it was a great idea and wanted to be included if the group met again. Her old friend Julie warned Shelly in a telephone call that she still was unable to control her emotions about the accident and felt she'd ruin it for everyone.

Shelly assured Julie that the purpose of the meeting was to help each other deal with whatever problems they might have. Peggy and John had accepted Shelly's invitation to come and stay overnight with the Landons.

Finally, the appointed day in mid-May dawned clear and

warm. They would gather around the pool where the wild for-sythia bloomed yellow against the gray fencing. Margo and Nancy had the event catered, so Shelly had little to do but show up. Shelly left Jake in charge at the club and had no worries about his being able to handle things there.

As arranged, people began arriving around two o'clock. It was such an emotional time, Shelly was glad Josh had offered to come. He was great at putting everyone at ease. There was small talk and getting re-acquainted. A few swam in the pool. When Peggy and John came, Peggy looked as if she were carrying a watermelon inside her tummy.

"Going to name it after you," Peggy said, glowing.

They ate at five, and at six Josh had them get into five groups for a time of just talking about what had happened to them two years ago and how their lives had changed. After that, they were to get into groups with people who had not yet heard their story and tell it again. He encouraged them to say the names of the loved ones they had lost. There was much emotional sharing.

By the end of the sessions, faces were unashamedly wet, but eyes looked peaceful and groups were holding hands. Then Josh quoted a Scripture passage, offered a prayer for each one, and softly began to sing, "I must tell Jesus. Jesus can help me. Jesus alone." Soon, the group joined in, and when it was over, everyone was hugging and laughing, most saying it was the best they had felt in two years.

Everyone was reluctant to leave, and it seemed they were talking even more freely about themselves after the sessions had ended. Shelly followed Josh inside the house as he prepared to leave. "You were wonderful, Josh," she complimented. "This could never have gone so well without you."

"You've done a worthwhile thing here tonight, Shelly. I'm proud of you. I just appreciate your letting me be a part of it." He smiled. "Good night."

Shelly felt excited about the future now. No holding back!

Feeling as if she could conquer the world, Shelly practiced for the aerobics contest with renewed vigor. She had no qualms about leaving Jake in charge of the health club while she was in Atlanta for a week. A young woman from Hendersonville came in, introduced herself as Loni, an aerobics instructor, and wanted to know if Shelly was going to Atlanta. She'd read about Shelly's health club in the Asheville *Citizen* and assumed Shelly would be going.

"What category are you entered in?" Shelly asked.

"High impact aerobics," Loni said. "I hope we're not in the same category."

Shelly laughed. "I was hoping the same thing. I'm entered in low impact. I'd thought of entering the high, but all my workers here say my individual routine works better in low impact, so I'm taking their word for it."

"Just getting a look at Mike Lacuna will be worth the trip."

"True," Shelly admitted with a smile. He was one of the judges. Shelly had seen articles and pictures of the handsome, fit young man numerous times. He was well-known for his aerobics show televised from Hawaii and seemed to be gaining in popularity.

Shelly and Loni made their plans to ride together. On Sunday afternoon, the first week in June, they headed down Interstate 40 West in Shelly's black Protege. Four hours later they arrived at the hotel in downtown Atlanta.

That evening at a welcoming party, they were introduced to the officials and judges. At one point, when Shelly returned to the punch island for a refill, a voice said in an accent definitely not southern, "Allow me, please."

She looked up into the flashing dark eyes and dazzling smile of Mike Lacuna. He lifted the ladle of punch and filled her cup. "Thank you, Mr. Lacuna. I'm Shelly Landon."

"Mike," he said, as he poured punch into his own cup. "Whatta delightaful atcent tu haf," he said and it was Shelly's turn to flash a broad smile and try hard to keep from laughing.

"It's southern. You're from Hawaii, right?" she asked as they moved aside slightly to make room for others to get to the island.

"Honolulu."

"I have a friend who lives on Oahu," she said. "You might know him. Trevor Steinbord."

Upon seeing Mike's slightly furrowed brow, she shrugged slightly. "He's a writer, so. . ."

"Oh, yes!" Mike said, brightening. "The name sounded familiar. I don't know him personally, but sure, he is very famous in Hawaii. But I have never read his books."

"Neither have I," Shelly admitted. "Actually, he's a friend of my family," she tried to explain, not wanting to give the impression that their relationship was something personal.

Seeing a look of renewed interest in his eyes at that declaration, she was glad the room was dimly lit, so he couldn't see her blush. Then one of the officials walked up. She smiled at Shelly, but took Mike by the arm. "Mike, there's someone I want you to meet."

"Nice meeting you, Shelly," he said, and they walked away.

"At least he remembered my name," Shelly said to Loni when she returned to the table.

"I was watching," Loni admitted. "You could have flirted a little more."

Shelly laughed. "If I can't do this on my ability, then I don't want it. But. . ." She turned mischievous eyes toward Loni. "If he weren't a judge, I might have flirted a little more."

For the rest of the week, group competitions were held and contestants were eliminated. Shelly had thought she might have an advantage because there weren't as many contestants in the low impact category as in the others. However, as the week wore on, she realized they were all competent. By Friday night, both Shelly and Loni were in the finals. The finals consisted of individual performances held at a university, and the public was invited. Shelly knew her parents, as well as Margo and Hanlan, would be there watching and praying for her.

She had worked out a low impact aerobic dance routine, utilizing not only the flexibility she'd gained from years of cheerleading, but also drawing on the grace and balance she'd obtained from early years of taking ballet lessons.

It occurred to her that her routine might be too much of a dance performance since many of the moves were beyond the abilities of an average aerobic-dance class. However, as her music began to play, she took on an entirely different frame of mind. The music "The Song from Moulin Rouge," had been her mother's suggestion, and Shelly felt it becoming a part of herself. She leaped into the circle formed by the spotlight and was lost to everything but the music and the routine she'd practiced hundreds of times.

Winning no longer mattered. Permeating her was the feeling of doing her best, accomplishing, competing, being a part of the flow of life. She knew, having watched videos of her own practicing, that the black leotard combined with her black hair provided a stark contrast with the fairness of her skin so that the lines of every move were shown to their best advantage.

There seemed to be nothing but the circle of light in which she performed and the long, thin shadow silhouetted against the floor and back wall that moved as she moved. She concluded with her hands lifted in a praising gesture, her head back and her body perfectly still so that the audience might see the human body in an artistic pose.

When the music ended, there was complete silence. Shelly felt as if she had ceased to breathe. Then as she slowly brought her hands down, the audience burst into spontaneous applause. She had done her best and didn't need further reward. Once again, she had learned that fulfillment comes in participating in life and giving of one's self.

&

"And the winner in the low impact aerobic dance category is. . .

Shelly Landon!"

The words and the applause were still ringing in her ears a week later. She could still feel the warm handshake of Mike Lacuna who said, "If you ever get to Hawaii, let me know. Perhaps you could be on my show."

She had felt that highly improbable, but it had been nice to hear and even contemplate. There had been media coverage at the competition, and as soon as she returned home, she discovered she was a local celebrity. Interviews, newspaper articles, TV appearances, and increased business resulted.

"I'd like to take you out to celebrate, Shelly," Jake said, and when she hesitated, he added quickly, "Please let me do this."

"One of us should be here at night, Jake. I can't ask the day manager to stay over."

He appeared thoughtful. "We could go Sunday night, say. . . to the Grove Park Inn."

"Jake, you took this job to make extra money."

"But you gave us all a ten percent raise when you got back from Atlanta, remember?"

"I don't want you spending it on me. Tell you what, let me at least pay my way."

"A deal," he said quickly, and Shelly thought he looked greatly relieved.

"We could go to a less expensive—"

He was shaking his head. "Nope. Put on your fancy duds and Grove Park it is."

When they got there, he led her to an open-air room at the back. Suddenly a crowd of people surrounded her, yelling, "Surprise!" Shelly stood in stunned silence. There were her parents, the Steinbords, workers from the health club, and several of her friends from church.

"Our Shelly has done a lot of things to be congratulated for," Hanlan Steinbord said, standing to speak to the guests gathered around the table where they could look out at the long, sloping lawn, the forest of lush green trees, and the towering mountain ranges beyond that, which formed a jagged greenish-purple horizon against a graying sky. "She's won a contest and turned a mediocre health club into a booming business. But most of all, she's making life a little better for a lot of people. She's very special."

Margo rose from her chair to stand beside Hanlan. "We're so proud of you, Shelly."

They lifted their glasses, and Philip Landon said, "Happy birthday, Shelly." The guests repeated his words and lifted their glasses in a toast to her.

Her birthday wasn't for three days, and she hadn't given it any thought. She stood and spread her hands helplessly. "I'm . . .speechless."

"Now, Shelly," her mother reprimanded, "no lying on your birthday."

Everyone laughed.

"Well, almost," Shelly admitted. "But every time I try to do something, I get rewarded, or praised, or thanked, or. . .thrown a party! Thank you so much."

Later, on the way home, Jake said, "Shelly, I want you to know how much I appreciate what you've done for me personally."

"Jake, I haven't done anything but give you a job. You're the one who has applied yourself in every way."

"No, you gave me confidence in myself. That goes a long way. And I just want you to know how much you mean to me."

Shelly felt a sinking feeling. She didn't want to hurt Jake's feelings. "Jake, you and I have become good friends, and we work well together, but. . ."

He laughed softly. "Hey, don't get me wrong. I'm not getting serious on you. I know, Shelly, you wouldn't even consider me in that way."

"Jake, why do you put yourself down that way?"

He shook his head. "I'm just being honest. I'm not in the same league as you. I'm just plain, basic Jake who's messed up his life in a lot of ways and you're. . .well, so beautiful and intelligent and always doing new and different things. You'd never settle down with a nobody like me. Now, isn't that the truth?"

"Well, not because there's anything wrong with you. I'm not interested in anybody, and I don't expect to be ever again."

"I want you to know that I admire you a lot."

"Jake, please," she pleaded.

"No, I'm not making moves on you. I'm saying this to let you know where I stand. I can tell you're going places—with your winning that contest and being asked to speak different places. I want you to know if you ever decide you need more help at the club, I'd gladly quit my job with Dad and be evening manager."

Shelly could only stare at him. She hadn't dreamed he would want to do that. All sorts of possibilities seemed to be pressing on her mind.

When she didn't reply to his statements, Jake became unsure again. "Do you suppose Mr. Steinbord would consider me as manager?"

"You mean Trevor?" she asked, somewhat surprised.

"Yeah."

"Oh, he wouldn't care," Shelly said. "He's not interested in the operation of it." She hadn't told Jake that she was part owner because if her word meant anything, she wasn't. She'd given it to Trevor.

But. . .the idea going through her mind made her shiver with anticipation. Or was it fear?

When she got home, she called the Steinbords and talked to Margo. "Thanks for the party," she said. "It was such a wonderful surprise. And I know you were behind it."

"You deserved it, darling," Margo said.

"Um, Margo, is it. . .night or day in Hawaii?"

She could tell Margo was surprised. "Well, let's see. It's. . . yes, it's day."

"Could you give me Trevor's telephone number?"

"Certainly! Hold on!"

In a few seconds she was back on the line with the number. Shelly knew Margo wouldn't ask, but would think it awfully weird that she wanted Trevor's number. Maybe she should seek Margo's advice. "I'm thinking of asking him to sell the health club to me. Is that. . .too far out?"

"Why, I think it's a marvelous idea." Margo sounded totally delighted. "Do let me know what he says. I couldn't possibly sleep tonight without knowing the answer."

Shelly picked up the receiver.

He probably wouldn't be home. She put it down again.

After taking a deep breath, she picked it up again. How in the world could she say, "Will you sell me the health club?" Why, he'd laugh her under the bed.

She decided to make a few notes on how to approach him. After studying them for a long time, she sighed heavily, picked up the phone, and dialed.

When it was answered on the other line, she said, "Margo, I've decided this can't be done by phone. I'll have to do it in person."

eleven

Trevor pushed the swivel chair away from his computer and walked to the window. His blue eyes swept across the balcony deck, which was surrounded by palms, flowering plants, ferns, and tall grasses. His gaze followed the twisting dirt path that disappeared into the lush foliage, leading to the white sands of his private beach. Beyond, the deep purple water merged with an azure Hawaiian sky. He looked up, as if to catch a glimpse of a jet high above the blue Pacific.

The mid-morning sun touched his bronzed skin and turned his blond hair to gold. He shoved his hands into his slacks pockets and leaned his tall frame against the window casing.

Shelly Landon was on her way to Hawaii!

But why?

A week ago, as if two years had not passed since he first extended the invitation, he received a postcard:

> *The Hawaiian vacation sounds terrific. Could you suggest a place to stay? I'm looking forward to doing the hula.*
>
> *Shelly*

Trevor had laughed, remembering how animated her face could be when she was excited. He rang her up. "I'll make all the arrangements," he said. "Just let me know your arrival time."

Now, he turned off his computer, opened his door bearing the DO NOT DISTURB sign, and found Maria in the kitchen, inspecting crystal candleholders.

She turned at the sound of his footsteps on the tile floor. "I know you like candlelight with your ladies," she said. A mischievous light in her black eyes accompanied her grin.

"Maria," Trevor reprimanded. "I warned you about remarks like that. Shelly Landon is not my lady. She was Don's girl."

"Ohhh." Maria's oriental face softened, and she touched his arm.

Trevor covered her hand with his and smiled down at her sympathetic expression. "That was almost three years ago, Maria. We've all gone on with our lives." A touch of frustration colored his voice. "But I don't know why she's coming here."

"What I know," Maria said with a pointed glance, "is that ever since you found out she's coming, you've been as jumpy as a frog that can't stay on his lily pad."

Inside, Trevor felt as quivery as a palm branch in a hurricane. However, he smiled at the woman who tried to take him under her wings. "She will probably say I'm a recluse, weird, and still, to use her phrase, 'Don's ogre brother'."

Maria gasped. "She said that?"

Trevor nodded.

She came to his defense. "Then she doesn't know you."

"And she never wanted to," he said, more to himself than Maria.

A little later, Trevor told Maria that he was leaving and drove away from his home that nestled against a hillside near the swank Kahala residential area.

After a twenty minute drive, he parked his light blue Porsche in the parking lot at the Honolulu International Airport, then went inside and bought a copy of the morning *Advertiser*. He had thirty-five minutes to wait.

❧

Shelly's stomach growled that it was meal time, but since they'd soon be landing, she'd rejected any food other than a miniature bag of toasted almonds and a cup of orange juice. She handed the flight attendant her empty glass, then twisted uncomfortably in the narrow seat, careful not to elbow the Japanese man who had sat beside her for hours, concentrating on documents with many numerical columns. She alternately lifted each shapely leg, bent forward slightly, and massaged her well-turned calves.

She had much to think about and didn't mind the lack of communication from her seatmate who had taken out his laptop as soon as they were in the air over Los Angeles.

She looked at her watch and realized she'd lost track of the number of times she'd set it back when they passed another time zone. The closer she came to Hawaii, the closer she came to the time she left North Carolina. If one judged life by the clock, it would seem that she was making no progress at all. But she didn't feel that she was going backward. This was one of the most forward steps she'd taken in three years.

She could not go on forever with Trevor as a silent partner who might return someday and claim the health club as his own. She must get something settled legally. She would try to find the right moment in which to confront Trevor and hope he would respond favorably rather than treat her like a child who isn't to be taken seriously.

Mentally preparing herself for the worst, she reminded herself that she had also written to Mike Lacuna that she would be in Hawaii the first week in July. He had offered to assist her in any way, but Shelly felt it best to leave the arrangements in Trevor's hands. Her family and the Steinbords would never understand if she refused Trevor's help. Also, at this point, she didn't want to offend him. She must remember to be cordial and sweet. Sweet?

She almost laughed aloud at the thought of being sweet to Trevor. Instead, she straightened and smoothed the skirt of her beige suit that fell neatly right above her knees.

Soon, she'd be in Hawaii. She closed her eyes against the feeling that rose from her stomach and toward her throat. This was not hunger, but a nervous reaction. She'd felt it on more than one occasion, and each time it had been when she was forced into an encounter with Trevor.

At that thought, she opened her eyes in time to see that a cloud cast a shadow across the window. She saw her face reflected and the uncertainty that lay in her eyes. Could she overcome her immature dislike for Trevor and face the situation squarely as an adult?

And Trevor? What kind of man was he? She'd seen the movie made of one of his books and thought it excellent, even though it was sad that the main character didn't get the girl he wanted. And he had incorporated a spiritual message. He obviously was having a good influence on the world, as her parents and the Steinbords had intimated many times. Maybe she had misjudged him.

Three years ago she hadn't been able to see him as an individual, and yet he had done a fine thing by encouraging her to work that summer in Haiti. But. . .had his success in the literary world made him an intellectual? What did it mean that he'd never married? He was certainly a good catch by the world's standards. Was it possible to meet Trevor on common ground and feel as close to him as she felt to the other members of the Steinbord family?

And too, how would he feel about her—a twenty-four-year-old woman whose degree in physical education had taken her no farther than a job in which she still kicked up her legs, swung her arms, stuck her rear in the air to stretch her hamstrings, and counted no higher than ten a hundred times a day?

In some people's eyes she had accomplished. . .*something*. She managed a health club, had started a successful program for the handicapped, had won a contest. But. . .it was still Trevor's health club, and it was his family who had made her accomplishments possible. Maybe, to a person with international success, hers would seem inconsequential.

Stop it! she told herself. Trevor Steinbord had always been the only person in the world who could make her feel so self-conscious. She must get over that!

A *dong* reached her consciousness, and she opened her eyes

to see the "Fasten Seatbelt" sign flash on. Relief and excitement washed over her as land appeared on the watery horizon. She took a mirror from her purse to inspect her black hair that was brushed back and twisted into a braided knot at the back of her head. She applied peach-colored gloss to her lips.

After they landed, the Japanese man smiled again and stood aside for her to go first. When she entered the airport, her eyes surveyed the waiting room and lit upon a blond head bent over a note pad. Well, that figured! Trevor was not even aware that she had arrived. He was more interested in whatever he was writing.

"Shelly!" he exclaimed, as if surprised when she walked up. He stood. "How good to see you. How was your flight?"

"Long," she replied and lifted the lei to enjoy the fragrance. She pretended ecstasy over the aroma and glanced up at him. Most of the times she'd seen him, he'd been dressed in a tux or a suit or dressy pants and shirt. That had influenced her decision to wear a suit and heels for this momentous occasion. Now he stood before her in casual attire: Dockers and a short-sleeved, colorful shirt. It underscored the fact that they were the two most incompatible people on earth.

"What were you writing?" she asked, wanting him to know she was slightly ticked off that he didn't even know she'd arrived until she was right in front of him.

He shrugged, tucking the small note pad in his shirt pocket. "Just an observation."

"About me?"

"You, Shelly?" he questioned. Then seeing the color rise to her face, he handed her the note pad.

She read:

> *James felt that crazy fever which threatened to destroy his brain when Eileen appeared in the doorway of the plane. Her beauty left him breathless. His attention turned, however, to others who viewed her similarly. Even the most staid of men looked upon*

> *her with fanciful imagination evident in their glow-*
> *ing eyes, as if they desired to offer her diamonds to*
> *grace her lovely neck.*

Shelly laughed. "So that's how you develop characters. By gross exaggeration. And where, may I ask, is this Eileen?"

His glance moved behind her. "Could be any of them."

Shelly shook her head but returned Trevor's warm smile, grateful for this exchange that alleviated her concern about an awkward first encounter in his territory.

"Come, 'James'," she jested with a lift of her chin. "Let's find my bag."

"Bag?" he questioned. "Singular?"

Shelly laughed. "Betsy and Katrina informed me that part of the fun of Hawaii is the shopping. So I brought the bare essentials."

"Mmmm," he said, stopping in his tracks. "That conjured up a vision of Eileen. . ."

Shelly impulsively reached up as if to prevent his taking out the note pad again but withdrew her hand before she could touch him.

He grasped her hand before it could fall to her side. "I'm only joking with you, Shelly. But seriously," he said, uncaring who passed by or heard, "I'm glad you're here."

His touch around her wrist was like an electric shock surging through her. But, she reminded herself, she was a mature Shelly, attempting to discover, appreciate, and understand other human beings who had their strengths and weaknesses—even if that other human being happened to be Trevor Steinbord.

Warmth emanated from Trevor's strong tanned fingers, and Shelly appreciated the effort he was making to keep things light and pretend they were life-long friends. She reminded herself of her purpose in being here. Her grin became a genuine smile, and she could honestly say. "I'm glad to be here, Trevor. Really."

He gently squeezed her hand, then released it.

After he found her bag and she was seated in the blue Porsche, it suddenly occurred to her that they were not moving. With a quick turn of her head, she saw that his face was directly across from hers and his sky-blue eyes looked into hers. She had never looked into his eyes long enough to try and discover what was there. Now she did—and found a strangely disturbing intensity.

❧

Trevor broke his gaze and started up the car. As he drove along the streets, he acted as tour guide. His spirits were buoyed beyond his wildest dreams. He'd touched her hand, welcomed her to Hawaii, spent at least five minutes with her already, and wonder of wonders, Shelly Landon hadn't bolted and run.

"Where will I be staying?" Shelly asked.

"You'll be staying at my house with my housekeeper and her husband. They act as caretakers, and Maria will be wanting to mother you on sight!"

"But I don't want to be kicking you out of your own home!" Shelly protested.

"Don't worry," Trevor reassured her. "I'll be staying in the guest house out back. I do that often anyway when I want to get away from the phone and other interruptions and get some serious writing done."

So far, so good! Trevor thought as he parked the blue Porsche under the deck.

❧

Shelly felt strangely euphoric. She got out of the car and walked along the path to the front steps, delightfully surveying the exotic foliage. Trevor stepped up beside her with her suitcase.

Her warm brown eyes met his. "It's everything your parents and mine said, Trevor," she complimented. "I can hardly wait to experience Hawaii. Especially the beach."

They ascended the steps and walked onto the deck. Trevor gestured toward the ocean. "Just follow the path, Shelly, and it will bring you to the private beach for Kahala residents and their guests. I want you to make yourself at home—like you always did at our house in North Carolina."

Shelly quickly recalled how the only time she hadn't felt at home with the Steinbords was when Trevor had been there. And now she was standing on his front deck and he had invited her into his home as if they were friends. As a fiction writer, pretending was his trade—but she'd never been any good at it.

She glanced up at him. "Thanks for inviting me, Trevor. But, I don't want you being kind to me for our families' sake."

"I think you owe me something, Shelly."

She lifted her chin. "I owe you something?" she asked with incredulity, then immediately remembered her resolve not to behave rudely with Trevor. She was not obligated to stay here. In fact, she had no obligations here except to herself. With that thought, her lips curved into a smile and a coyness crept into her eyes. "Rent!" she said with a laugh. "How much? How much do I owe you for two-weeks rent? That is, supposing I stay."

Trevor pretended consternation. "At least see the accommodations. You might find them totally unsuitable at any price."

"The ocean has already influenced me," she said coyly.

"Then I offer a blanket and you can camp out on the beach."

"You're tempting me."

"Really?" he jested, lifting an eyebrow. "I thought I only antagonized you." He opened the screen door and motioned for her to enter.

Shelly passed in front of him with a shake of her head. She wasn't about to touch that line, but a funny feeling swirled around inside at the thought of Trevor Steinbord being a temptation to her. It must be jet lag or Hawaiian air or something that let a thought like that cross her mind. Trevor considered her nothing more than an immature girl who happened to be friends with his family. She turned toward him as he stepped into the foyer and the screen door closed behind him.

She regarded him skeptically. Since she'd increased business threefold at the health club was he looking for a percentage of the profits? "What did you mean, that I owe you something, Trevor?"

"Well," he began in a serious tone, "now that we're both adults it's time to stop pretending we're strangers. We've known each other all our lives, and yet we've stayed out of each other's way. I'd like to know, once and for all, if my *hamartia* is something you can never accept or tolerate."

"Is that something like. . .halitosis?"

"Can't brush it away," he said and laughed.

"I'm not an intellectual, Trevor. Just an aerobics instructor." Her voice held a twinge of exasperation. He knew, of course, that her major claim to fame was being an ex-cheerleader. "What on earth is your hammer. . .hammar. . .?"

"Hamartia," he finished for her. "It originated in Greek mythology and is embodied in their literature," he continued, putting on an exaggerated formal tone that made him sound like some British diplomat. "Hamartia is a fatal flaw that eventually leads to one's decline and inevitable downfall."

Shelly laughed. "You're definitely a hoity-toity intellectual if I ever heard one." A slight uneasiness swept over her as she realized she was laughing with Trevor. He'd joked before, but she'd never thought him funny.

"In the words of a commoner," he said, "which you know I am—it's time Shelly Landon faced, examined, defined, and declared why she never liked Trevor Steinbord, and if, in her opinion, he's a hopeless case."

"That was childish," she quietly admitted, surprised he would so bluntly approach the subject when she'd been determined to skirt around it. "I think you're right. We're both mature enough to realize that everyone in the world cannot be friends. Sometimes, not even within family relationships." She grinned and said playfully, "But I seriously doubt that you are inflicted with an incurable fatal flaw. You don't appear to be suffering."

She had always taken for granted the incredibly attractive Steinbord family of blue-eyed blonds. However, her main attachment had been to Don, so Trevor's attractiveness had never been an issue for her. Why now? She answered the question immediately. *Because Don's death has made us all more acutely aware of living in harmony with those around us. Because Trevor and I are away from family and should face our differences.*

"While we're being honest," she began in a serious tone, "let me say that I have an ulterior motive in coming to Hawaii. But I'll tell you about that later."

"Then it wasn't my charm?" he asked, pretending chagrin. "I'll have to live with the disappointment, but I think I'll survive. Now let's get you and your suitcase to your room. Straight ahead." He nodded toward the hallway, and Shelly walked ahead of him, hoping that she hadn't made the biggest mistake of her life by trying to meet Trevor Steinbord on his own turf.

twelve

Trevor gestured toward the front room on the right. "Living room." His head turned toward the room on the left. "My office."

Shelly read the "DO NOT DISTURB" sign and was reminded anew that she'd never read a word he'd written. *Hamartia* just might be a disease inflicting her, rather than him, for she'd never been willing to examine the truth, the reality, of her reticent and sometimes hostile feelings toward him. Now, she rather welcomed the possibility of ridding herself of that burden. How refreshing it would be for their families to get together without her being nervous about Trevor.

They came to the second door on the right. "This is the guest bedroom. Directly across from Maria and Graggy Galali's suite." Trevor set her suitcase inside. "If you need anything during the night, they'll be more than happy to help you."

Golden rays of the mid-afternoon sun invaded the room from the two windows on the outside wall and slanted across the multi-colored quilt spread over the king-size bed. Shelly walked across the hardwood floor, stepped onto the oriental rug, and tested the mattress with her fingers.

"How inviting," she said and looked over her shoulder at Trevor. "Do you realize it's the middle of the night in North Carolina?"

Before he could do more than nod assent, she saw the orchid on the pillow and picked it up. "Oh, how pretty." She turned to face him, her voice soft when she added, "and thoughtful."

"I would like to take full credit," Trevor said with some trepidation, "but Maria is the thoughtful one. It's apparently

127

from out back."

Shelly returned the orchid to the pillow, then sat on the side of the bed.

Trevor smiled. "Let's meet Maria."

They passed by the dining room doorway. "That's where we will have dinner, so I'll show it to you later." They walked on to the kitchen.

"Maria," Trevor called, entering the room. The woman turned to face them, a knife in one hand and a piece of celery in the other. Trevor introduced them.

Shelly immediately went over and thanked Maria for the orchid, reported her famished state of being, her tense muscles from lack of exercise, her inability to stay awake a moment longer, and the attack of jet lag that dulled her senses.

Maria assured her that dinner would be ready in less than two hours, no she didn't need help, and that Shelly should make herself at home. "You did not tell me," Maria reprimanded Trevor, "how beautiful she is. And nice."

Shelly glanced at Trevor as if to say, "You didn't?"

He hid a smile behind his hand and cleared his throat.

"I'm preparing a special dinner for you," Maria said proudly.

It took will power, but Shelly said she'd wait.

A breakfast bar separated the cooking area from the informal eating area, which was surrounded by windows on one side and sliding glass doors on another. The windows provided a view of lush foliage on the right and the patio on the left and the back. It was the most modern-looking part of the house.

"Dad remodeled the kitchen," Trevor said.

Shelly nodded. "I recognize the style. He likes to open rooms up to nature."

Trevor opened the sliding glass doors and they stepped onto the patio. "You might like to rest out here awhile before dinner."

"Let me change first. I can't stand this suit a minute longer. I feel like I've worn it for days. Ohhh, these shoes too."

Shelly hurried inside, stepped out of the high heels and threw the suit over a chair. She rummaged through the suitcase and put on a pair of shorts and a T-shirt. Barefooted, she hurried back to the patio, then sank into the nearest lounge chair.

Trevor sat a few feet away.

"This is truly a paradise, Trevor," she complimented. "Thanks for inviting me. I mean that sincerely."

He spread his hands. "I'm offering you my hospitality, just the way my family has done since the day you were born. I hope you'll like it here."

"You couldn't budge me out of this chair with a crowbar," she kidded, to cover the strange sensation of having a cordial conversation with Trevor. "But," she said, recalling how much time he'd spent on his writing, even as a young man, "I don't want to infringe upon your time. You must have a writing schedule or something." His parents always talked about his burning the midnight oil. Katrina and Betsy accused him of having a love affair with typing paper.

"Yes, but this is a time of research, absorption, and note-taking, more than actual creativity. I allow myself flexibility until I get into the actual work on a book."

Shelly yawned. "Oh, excuse me."

"Why don't you take a nap? We could move that chair over into the shade. As inviting as the sun may seem, it's best to limit your exposure. Get a tan slowly."

"That sounds like a wonderful idea," Shelly said and quickly got up to move the chair. "Would you call me about thirty minutes before dinner? I want to clean up a little. I'm such a grunge."

"I'll call you," he said and smiled down at her.

Shelly looked up and met his gaze. Why did he study her so? What did he really think of her? Before she could reach any conclusions, Trevor nodded at her and went back into the house.

Resolutely, Shelly closed her eyes, determined to sleep. But she didn't nap immediately. She attributed her wakefulness to a combination of things: fatigue and tension mixed with excitement and anticipation. She had always ignored Trevor or pushed him away. Now she was determined to rise to the challenge of discovering this man, to explore her past animosity toward him, and to try to be civil enough so that they could work out some business deal for the health club.

It had been more than twenty-four hours since she'd done more than doze. She gave in to the fatigue, drifted away, and it seemed almost immediately that someone was calling her name, trying to bring her back.

&

"Shelly."

Trevor spoke her name as if she were a figment of his imagination and might disappear if he spoke too loudly.

While she slept, he'd gone in to change and wondered if he had wanted something like this so desperately he had confused reality with imagination and would return to the patio to find an empty chair, with only his subconscious to laugh and sneer at him for being such a dreamer.

She did not disappear. Instead she raised her arms above her head and stretched out her sleek, beautiful body. She appeared lost somewhere between oblivion and consciousness.

Her lips were slightly parted. That's how she slept. He'd seen that manifested all over the Steinbord house. When she was a toddler, she'd often fallen asleep on the floor in front of the TV. Later, she'd fallen asleep by the pool and he'd have to call her so she wouldn't burn.

He'd seen her sleepily walk down the hallway in a robe or in a long T-shirt. But he'd never used any excuse to touch her. He'd never shaken her awake, nor reached out his hand—not since her mother had warned him about the soft spot on her head when she was a newborn. It was as if she were fragile. He mustn't touch her because she was an innocent baby and he a growing boy. He mustn't because she was a teenager and he a man. He mustn't because she belonged to his brother. The time came when he had to admit it was not Shelly who was fragile—but himself.

Even now, as a thirty-two-year-old man who made a living exploring, explaining, understanding, and questioning human nature and could evoke identification from his reading audience, he could stand before Shelly and be reduced to the state of a quaking fledgling writer under the scrutiny of the world's greatest critic.

He smiled at the irony of it. Shelly had been his most severe personal critic. And he, an expert with words, had never been able to impress her with a single one. Perhaps he should write her a letter. That way he could revise and re-write and perfect it and make her understand what he was all about.

Ah, but he'd already done that. She was there in his books. She'd simply never cared enough to read them. And now, this expert with words could hardly whisper her name.

"Shelly."

ॐ

Slowly her eyes swept upward. For an instant they questioned, as clearly as if she had spoken the words, "What on earth are you doing here, Trevor Steinbord?"

"Maria says dinner will be ready soon."

"Oh, thanks." She realized he had changed his clothes. "I need to shower and change, if there's time."

"There is—half an hour, as requested, my lady." Trevor's eyes glinted with mischief.

Shelly jumped up and hurried back to her bedroom. She took a quick shower in the attached bathroom and then changed into dressy slacks, a cream-colored blouse, and sandals. Glancing at her watch she realized she was just under the allotted time when she emerged from the bedroom and went out to join Trevor on the patio.

The gentle breeze, like fingers, lifted the strands of her black hair, crimped from having been inhibited by the braid, and spread them to dance on the wind. Her gold earrings caught the sun. She stopped in front of him and raised her face that had matured into more clearly defined lines during the past few years.

Her eyes closed. Her long black lashes, slightly curled on the ends, lay above the blush on her cheeks. The nostrils of her perfectly-shaped nose twitched slightly as she inhaled deeply. Her rosy lips smiled and the warm brown of her eyes held a dreamy expression. "That food smells heavenly. I can't wait a minute longer."

Trevor gestured mutely toward the back door.

"This is wonderful, Trevor," Shelly said, looking up at him after he seated her at the dining room table. "But you don't need to be formal with me."

"Just extending Hawaiian hospitality," he protested as Maria entered the dining room with the first course.

❧

Trevor could hardly tell Shelly what he was really feeling. He knew how she'd respond if he told her that he wanted to be able to treasure the memory of her sitting across from him in his dining room. He wanted to watch her, to recall the picture of her as she walked out onto the patio, ready for their first private dinner together.

So many years had passed with her sitting beside Don at their dining room table in North Carolina. He'd shared her with family, the view of the golf course outside the picture window in the dining room, other guests—all sorts of distractions. Conversations with other people always occupied her mind and time. She'd never cared to have a conversation with him. He'd sat silent, occasionally making a remark that she apparently thought too intelligent or too ridiculous or too unrelated to bother with.

Tonight was his. The memories would be his to use as he wished. If it didn't work for him personally, he could enhance the evening in a book. That's how he made things work—one way or another.

Trevor always preferred a late dinner, with the light from the chandelier providing its soft glow. He felt conversations flowed better when the outside world lay dark beyond the windows and there were no distractions from the enjoyment of good food and the companionship of his dinner guests.

He could leave the table as it was tonight: small, round, and in the center of the room. Or he could add one or two leaves, making it more like a conference table where he could spread out his manuscripts for an editor, agent, or his own revisions.

He'd often wondered, and had been asked by interviewers, if as a bachelor in his early thirties, he'd become set in his ways and might find change difficult. Their meaning of "change" implied taking a wife. He replied that if the right woman came along, he'd welcome whatever change came with her.

Deep within, he wasn't quite so certain and wondered if he really had become set in his ways. Most of his relationships were in accordance with his convenience and preferred schedule. Today was a challenge for him, and he found himself not set in his ways at all, but looking forward to this late-afternoon dinner with Shelly Landon. The drapes were drawn across the windows to obscure the glare of the sun's slanting rays, lending a certain aura of intimacy to the room.

It was not intimacy, however, that manifested itself, but the warm, friendly attitude that had characterized Shelly's personality toward everyone but him for as long as he could remember. While squeezing lemon into her iced tea, scattering vinaigrette over her fresh island salad, buttering her pita bread, and testing the teriyaki chicken, she kept Maria in the dining room by asking questions and soon discovered Maria's entire life history.

Maria had lived on Maui until she met Graggy Galali, married him, and moved to Oahu. They'd reared six children. They lived at Trevor's estate and looked after it while he was away on business, but their own home was occupied by their daughter Lula, who was divorced and had two small children. The arthritic Graggy now did odd jobs in the neighborhood as well as taking care of gardening and repairs for Trevor.

"Any good places to shop around here?" Shelly asked. "I've already used up the wardrobe I brought with me, except my swimsuit and formal dress."

Trevor looked on, pleased, as Shelly and Maria laughed together. Maria then gave a run-down on shopping places she knew well. "Oh, but you want to go to the Royal Hawaiian Shopping Center. It is six and one-half acres of anything you could want. My Lula works in one of the stores and she can get discounts. If I didn't have to work tomorrow," Maria said with a glance toward Trevor, who was silently eating his dinner, "I could take you shopping. A good time would be in the morning when he does his writing and doesn't like to be disturbed."

With such a condemnation of his unyielding schedule, which he would have gladly forgone to take Shelly shopping, and the expectant eyes of the women staring at him, Trevor had little alternative but to give in.

"You two can take the Porsche," he offered. "And, Shelly, I've already made reservations for a luau Friday night, in case you want to go. You might keep that in mind when you're shopping."

"Oh, great. That's one thing I was determined not to miss. What do you wear to a luau?"

"I know what to do," Maria assured, nodding. "We will go to the shops and dress you out Hawaiian style." She leaned down to Shelly's ear and whispered, "Something to knock his socks off."

Shelly laughed with Maria and lifted a forkful of chicken. "This is delicious, Maria."

She stole a glance at Trevor and felt a warmth rise to her cheeks. She had never even mildly flirted with him. Now, with his self-composed, tolerant expression over her and

Maria's whispering, she thought such an idea would be as impossible to him as to her.

A man like him probably didn't want his socks knocked off. But what kind of man was he, really? She'd never taken the time to find out. She simply fed upon her impressions from early childhood. She certainly had to respect the fact that he was young to have already become successful in his field, particularly in the creative arts. And too, there was his involvement with the mission program.

If he were a different Trevor, and she a different Shelly, and they had never met, she would be attracted to him. Strange that she should even notice that. She'd always known and taken for granted that the Steinbords were incredibly attractive persons. Margo had even had a reasonable amount of success as a film actress before she gave it up in favor of family life.

Both Katrina and Betsy were extraordinarily beautiful. Both had been beauty queens in college and had gravitated toward local modeling, but they had never tried to pursue a career that focused on their beauty, and it had not affected their egos. Don had been muscular and ruggedly handsome like his father. She'd taken it for granted that Trevor's good looks were was simply hereditary. It would have been uncharacteristic to belong to such a family and not be extraordinary in many ways.

The unusual thing about Trevor, however, was that he didn't follow the pattern of his family members. How had he come to be so different, she wondered. Even as a teenager, his literary goals exempted nights out with the boys or the girls. He had seemed introverted, while the rest of his family were definitely extroverts.

Strange that she should even want to know some of the answers to what made Trevor tick. She quickly attributed this to the fact that he was playing host to her and being excessively polite.

Trevor had not heard what Maria whispered to Shelly, but he did notice the tiny laugh that had escaped Shelly's throat. She regarded him with brief scrutiny. That was refreshing. Back home, he'd felt like a piece of furniture that she invariably tripped over.

"Maria has really taken to you, Shelly," he said warmly. "But that doesn't surprise me. You've always been a warm, caring person."

"Well, I guess my parents can take the credit for that."

The conversation turned to their families and what was happening in their lives. "My dad's more energetic than ever," Shelly reported. "He'd always been healthy, but since his heart attack, he's more careful of what he eats and does. He's back to being full-time at the hospital and says he feels better than he ever has in his life."

The others were about the same as always, with children growing like weeds. "Seems like yesterday you were scrambling after the toddler Betsy," Trevor recalled. "Now, she's expecting her second child."

"Next month," Shelly added. "I'll have to be there for that event!"

She'd just arrived, and already he had to face her leaving. "How long do you plan to stay?"

"I. . .I haven't planned." She turned her attention to her iced tea and picked up the glass.

Depends upon how well we get along? Trevor wondered.

After a sip and a thoughtful moment, she admitted, "I have some serious thinking to do."

Trevor's heart skipped a beat. *About her ulterior motive?*

"Oh, and I've got to make some phone calls."

"There's a phone in your room," Trevor told her. "I suppose you should call your parents and let them know you arrived all right, now that it won't be the middle of the night in North Carolina."

"I'll do that too," Shelly said, smiling at Maria who returned to the dining room and headed her way with a pitcher of iced tea. "But before it gets too late, I want to call Mike Lacuna."

"Who?" Maria almost dropped the pitcher.

"Mike Lacuna," Shelly repeated.

"Not *the* Mike Lacuna!" Maria exclaimed.

Shelly laughed. "I guess you know him."

Trevor shook his head, totally bewildered, and admitted to himself he'd already learned a few things about his own housekeeper that he hadn't known before. What now?

Maria refilled Shelly's glass, then set the pitcher on the table and, with eyes sparkling like Christmas lights, lifted her arms and flexed her biceps. "Oh, he has muscles and jumps around on all the beaches. When he jumps around, my heart goes thumpity-thump-thump!"

"That's what he does best," Shelly said, squeezing lemon into her iced tea. "Accelerates the heart rate."

Maria laughed. Trevor did not. "What is he?" he asked. "A kangaroo or something?"

Maria came to Mike's immediate defense. "Oh, he's a muscle man. You should see him." She addressed Shelly. "Oh, the way you look, I'll bet you jump like that too."

Shelly nodded, grinning. "He invited me to come here and exercise with him."

"And you said, 'Sure, I'll catch the next flight over'!" Trevor said, trying to joke.

Shelly laughed and explained, "On his TV program."

Maria's eyes glistened. "Will he come here to our beach?"

Shelly shrugged. "I don't know what he has planned. I need to call him right after dinner," she said. "I should have already." Shelly scattered vinaigrette dressing over a second helping of fresh island salad then glanced at Trevor. "You really don't know him?"

Trevor shook his head, and Maria explained, "He's in his office typing away when Mike comes on."

"Anyway," Shelly said, between bites, "I met Mike a few months ago in Atlanta at an aerobics contest. Incidentally, I won in my category."

"Yes, I heard," Trevor said. "And Mom sent me newspaper clippings. But I'd really like to hear all about it."

Shelly felt a little self-conscious about what appeared to be his genuine interest. She told him about it and about winning. "Mike was one of the judges, and he invited me to be on his show if I ever came to Hawaii. So! Here I am. You won't have to bother with me much at all. I expect to be quite busy. That's. . .one of my motives for coming to Hawaii."

So that was Shelly's motive. But this was the second time she'd mentioned motives, plural. He had the distinct feeling her motive involved him somehow, or was that just wishful thinking? He supposed he'd know soon enough what it might be—if he didn't allow her to get away. And it wasn't as if he had thought for a moment, just because he'd heard she didn't seem serious about Jake Simmons, that there weren't at least a dozen other men waiting on the sidelines.

Recalling Maria's remark about taping locations, Trevor said, "Lacuna's welcome to tape on Kaluha if he'd like."

Shelly's forkful of salad halted on the way to her mouth. "You mean that?"

He took a sip of iced tea, frowned at the glass, then looked directly into Shelly's surprised brown eyes. "I always mean what I say. You're my guest, Shelly. Your friends are welcome here."

She swallowed the bite of salad. "That's really nice of you, Trevor. Thanks. I'm really intent on seeing what Hawaii has to offer, enjoying it," she said, reverting to her usual jovial mood, "and living dangerously." Her eyes twinkled with mischief.

Trevor knew that she wasn't serious, but her lighthearted comment did imply that she was searching for independence. Hadn't he always told himself what he wanted most for

Shelly was for her to be settled and happy? Yes. . .that's what he'd told himself, but. . .

"Does 'living dangerously' mean you're ready for Maria's wickedly rich strawberry mousse on a graham cracker crumb crust?" he asked.

"Oh, dear," Shelly said weakly. "I ate so much chicken. Do you think she'll be offended if I save the dessert for later?"

"You praised her culinary efforts. However, I did warn her that you're into physical fitness and might eat like a bird."

"Instead," Shelly quipped, "I ate the bird! Just about the whole thing."

Trevor laughed and laid his napkin beside his plate as Maria came in to clear the table.

Shelly gave lavish compliments on the dinner, but insisted she couldn't eat another bite.

"Would you like to walk on the beach, sit on the patio or deck, or go somewhere?" Trevor asked.

Shelly pushed her chair back. "Sounds like I have a big day tomorrow." She smiled at Maria. "So, I'd like the walk along the beach. The exercise is a necessity at this point." She patted her full tummy. "But it was worth it."

She stood, and so did Trevor. "Oh, yes, I need to make those phone calls first," Shelly recalled and hurried off to her room.

When Trevor neared her bedroom door a short while later, Shelly apparently had already called her parents. She had a particular lilt to her voice when she exclaimed, "Mike! This is Shelly Landon. Oh, well, great! Yes, I just got here this afternoon."

She laughed, "That must have been uncomfortable."

Trevor looked toward the ceiling and shook his head. Apparently the jumper said he'd been sitting by the phone or maybe even on pins and needles—surely not waiting with bated breath! "Oh, you want to start tomorrow?"

The guy was wasting no time. Trevor stepped up and leaned against the casing of her bedroom door. She sat on the edge of the bed, her legs crossed, her shoes off. One foot swung freely. She held the phone against her ear and her head was tilted slightly back, revealing a delighted expression.

He wasn't surprised at whatever compliments the person on the other end of the line was giving her. Shelly was a beautiful young woman. Single. Extroverted. Warm. Caring. And she had a lovely body enhanced by many years of exercise.

Shelly glanced toward the doorway, ceased her foot motion, and looked uncertain.

Trevor walked in, holding out his hand. "May I?"

"Um, Mike?" She cleared her throat. "Trevor wants to say something to you."

Trevor ignored the distress in her eyes which told him she thought he was about to do something horrendous. "Lacuna?" he began cordially. "Yes, I am that one. Well, thanks. That's the kind of compliment a writer likes to hear."

Shelly was even more surprised when Trevor quickly changed the subject and said, "What is this about your taking my guest away and filming?" He listened for a while, and then asked, "Have you ever filmed at Kalula?"

Within the next few minutes, it was all set. The filming would be done on Kalula, and since Mike liked to tape a week's show within a few days in the same location, Trevor said that would be fine. He did, however, inform Mike that Shelly had an engagement the following morning, so it was arranged that Mike would come on Wednesday morning at eight o'clock. He and his crew were invited to use Trevor's house in whatever way they wanted or needed. And Trevor's modest replies indicated that Mike Lacuna thought Trevor was someone quite special. Shelly was impressed with Trevor's taking charge like that and being so generous with his home and his beach.

"We're just regular people here, Mike," he said. "Ask Shelly. She's known me all her life. I'm looking forward to meeting you."

He handed the phone to Shelly who quickly ended the conversation and caught up with Trevor who had walked from the room and headed toward the front entrance.

"That was so nice of you, Trevor."

"I told you that earlier."

"Yes, but I. . .wasn't sure you meant it."

Trevor wondered what he'd done—throwing her into the arms of another man. No. . .that sort of decision was her choice to make.

"Mike is so excited about taping here. And he wants to bring a book for you to autograph."

"I'll be happy to."

"By the way," she asked, "what do you do for exercise?"

He wondered if she thought him in shape. "Run. Swim. Walk. Work out in my gym."

"*Your* gym?"

He nodded. "Downstairs."

"Why didn't you show it to me?"

"I. . .just hadn't gotten around to it."

"You should know I would want to see that."

He lifted an eyebrow quizzically.

As they walked along the beach, Shelly asked about Trevor's career. He described the progress he'd made during the past two years. Since *Stifled* had been a success, both as a novel and a movie, another of his books was in the process of being filmed and the one with Haiti as a background was being considered for filming.

"I did see the film *Stifled.*"

He'd known she'd seen it, not with their families, but with Jake Simmons.

"It was excellent, of course," she said, as if that should be taken for granted, "and refreshing for a movie to have morals and people of. . ." She looked over at him uncertainly. "I'm not much of a critic," she admitted.

He grinned. "You're doing fine."

"Well, it had meaning."

"But. . . ?" he prompted.

"Your older man was such an admirable person. But I wondered if he was really a. . ."

Trevor stopped walking. "A what?"

"A. . .coward." Trevor knew he hadn't successfully hidden his reaction when Shelly closed her eyes and said, "Oh, dear, I've insulted you."

"No!" he said immediately, although he had to admit he'd never heard this criticism before. The critics agreed that the book had tremendous power and impact and understanding of the emotional deprivation of a creative mind. The world had praised his rendering of such a noble, self-sacrificing character. Such a personality was the basic underlying theme of all his books.

"I really want to know what you mean by that," Trevor said.

"He should have told the girl he loved her," Shelly explained with some trepidation.

Trevor shook his head. "He showed it."

"He showed it like a father or a doting uncle would. She had no idea he was in love with her."

Trevor tried to explain. "The point of the whole book is that the older man prevents her from having to choose. She can accept the love of the younger man without any regrets."

"But she didn't know she had a choice."

"Her love shouldn't be based on whether or not the older man loved her. It should only be based on her own feelings."

Shelly was thoughtful. "Maybe. But I suppose that depends on the viewer. I don't have the same definition of love that I had before Don died. Then, I wouldn't even consider an older man. Now, I would be grateful if I could fall in love. Age wouldn't be much of a consideration."

"A good point," Trevor agreed. "But look at my heroine. She did not have the experiences you now have. She would not look at life and the older man the way you do."

"Maybe you're right," Shelly conceded. "I would prefer Romeo and Juliet to get together too, but then the story might never have been a success."

They laughed together. But Trevor looked off into the distance. *My noble characters. . . cowards?*

Shelly's gaze followed Trevor's to the horizon where rays of the setting sun peeked out between orange and yellow clouds and sprinkled the water with gold.

"Now, tell me about yourself," he prompted and she turned away from the majestic ocean. They walked along the secluded beach where green palms swayed against a dark blue sky.

"Didn't your parents tell you what I'm doing at the health club?"

"Yes, but I'd like to hear your version."

Trevor watched as a light came into her dark eyes. Her gaze moved across the ocean, beyond the horizon, as she related her progress both at the club and personally. "Everyone has been encouraging me to take a vacation for quite a while."

"You've worked too hard?" he asked. "Are you not satisfied there?"

"Oh yes, I love it. And I'm beginning to think more in terms of my future than when I first took on the club."

"Which is?" he encouraged, when she looked down at her toes attempting to embed themselves in the soft white sand. He noticed that her toenails were polished red, but he didn't allow the smile he felt to reach his lips. She might think him less than serious about the conversation.

She shrugged. "When I first took on the club I concentrated on just getting through each day. Passing time. Trying to keep my mind occupied by reaching out to others. Now," she said as she began to walk again, "an idea has been playing around in my mind for quite some time." She looked up at him, wondering if this was the time to mention her plan. This comraderie between them couldn't last. She might not have another chance. She looked up at him. "It may not be workable."

"Does this have something to do with your ulterior motive?"

"Yes." She looked a little sheepish. "It may be totally unrealistic."

"Most of our greatest inventions seemed unrealistic, Shelly," Trevor reminded her. "The horseless carriage, talking machines, flying machines, and even more unrealistic, man on the moon. . ."

"My idea may be foolish," she began uncertainly.

"I've had enough bad ideas to fill the ocean." He stretched out his hand toward the vast expanse of water. "But after thought, revision, listening to my own instincts, and paying attention to the suggestions of an editor, those bad ideas could be changed, expanded, or deleted in favor of others. So," he continued, "tell me about it, and we'll see if we can make it work."

"You're actually giving me confidence, Trevor."

He grinned. "Part of my life's philosophy," he said. "All things are possible."

Shelly began to tell him of her work with the handicapped and her ideas that would expand service in that area. "I would like to start a newsletter," she said. "To help the handicapped become healthier in all ways—socially, emotionally, and spiritually, as well as physically."

His interested glance indicated she should continue as they walked side by side along the water's edge. She became absorbed in expressing her dreams to Trevor. "But I'm talking too much," she said suddenly. "Oh, the sunset's going to be gorgeous, isn't it?"

Her eyes were drawn to the horizon, where rays of the setting sun peeked out between orange and yellow clouds and tipped the water with sprinkles of gold. She turned with a dance-step, delighted with the scenery.

Trevor felt an incredible breathlessness. He saw the glimmer of awe in her eyes as she viewed the setting sun behind him. The orange of the sunset glinted like flames in her brown eyes. When she turned to face him, her hair spread out like a fan, reminding him of the night he'd taken her to the senior dance and she'd turned from him. This time, she faced him. An over-whelming instinct washed over him. He fought hard to relegate it to the character of Eileen and forced himself to exercise the self-control that he'd learned to use around Shelly. She was communicating with him, but she still wasn't sure of him enough to reveal whatever plan had brought her to Hawaii.

"I suspect," he said, "the sunset is going to be one of our most beautiful. We can watch it from the deck if you'd like."

Shelly nodded, and they headed back toward the house.

After they reached the deck, Maria brought their dessert, a pot of coffee, and two cups.

"Join us, Maria," Shelly invited.

"Thank you, but I'll be heading off to our suite, if that's all right."

Trevor said it was and thanked her again for the wonderful meal.

Shelly finished her mousse, accepted the coffee Trevor poured for her, then sat back, staring at the view. The clouds turned brown and the sky turned orange.

Trevor observed Shelly as she watched the changing sky. He'd never known her to be so quiet. Finally, she spoke. "This is so peaceful, Trevor. It must be a perfect place for thinking. For a long time I didn't want to think. But time. . .really does help."

Her finger traced a circle around the rim of her coffee cup. Trevor reached over and took her hand in his. He gently squeezed it and said, "I understand." Before she had time to withdraw, he moved his hand away and looked out as the navy blue water and sky met to swallow the sun, leaving behind a tongue of orange-red horizon. Remembering the feel of Shelly's fingers against his, he was afraid to hope that she might finally be seeing him as a friend. And if she had put her animosity behind, would she ever be willing to be more than a friend?

꙳

Shelly glanced at her hand resting idly on the table, then her eyes moved to his hand. The Steinbord men had large hands. Trevor's fingers were long and slender with carefully groomed nails. Golden hairs curled on his tanned arm. She had not resented his touch, rather found it. . . Her mind stopped. The word *comforting* didn't seem to fit. She couldn't find a word that described the touch. Why had he done it? Strangely, she found herself wanting to know this man she'd been around all her life but did not in the least understand.

The mountains of North Carolina had surrounded her with a kind of security, like the families who had loved and protected her. Her vision now expanded to a horizon that seemed limitless, as if the world were open to her for discovery.

"Maybe we could be friends, Trevor." When he glanced away and turned his head slightly from her to gaze toward the palms swaying in the light breeze like wings fluttering beneath the moonlight, she worried if she had misspoken.

He was silent for so long that Shelly wondered if he had perhaps lapsed into thinking about his writing, but then he said, "I hope you can consider me a friend, Shelly."

Shelly felt uncomfortable for the first time since she'd arrived, but it wasn't because of Trevor. It was because of herself. Friendship could not be be based on dishonesty. And how many times had Trevor indicated he wanted honesty from her—even if it included her dislike of him? He had given no indication that he had any motive toward her other than friendship. And since he knew her so well, he would not be fooled by her waiting for the "right moment" to mention a business deal.

"Trevor," she began tentatively, despite her fatigue and

trepidation. "The reason I decided to come to Hawaii is to talk to you about the health club."

His nod and questioning gaze encouraged her to continue.

"I wondered if we could work out a deal for me to buy the health club from you?"

He rose, walked over to the railing, and held onto it, as she explained. "You don't seem to really care about the health club. I know it's yours, since I gave you my half, so I'm willing to buy the whole thing from you. Of course, I don't have much money, but I thought since you don't really need the money, you might let me make payments that aren't too steep. Or if you want me to get a loan, then Mom and Dad would do that and let me pay them. There are many possible ways of doing this, and of course you're the one to decide that."

She paused, and when he didn't turn toward her or make any comment, she began talking again. "But if you want to keep it for sentimental reasons, since Gran left it to you, that's understandable. And if you don't want to sell it, then I'd appreciate your letting me know where I stand—that is, if you feel the whole thing is yours since I gave it to you. If you don't, then we need to make things clear between us. As it stands now, sometimes I think, 'Why am I doing all this?' At any time you might come and claim the club, and where does that leave me? So we need to legally clarify our arrangement. This is my career and future, and I'm not always sure which way to go. I do have plans for more improvements and expansion, and I'm being asked to speak to various groups, particularly the handicapped. I'd like more involvement with them, but it wouldn't be right to set up a lot of programs. You might come back and not want that, and where does that leave them? But my parents and your family knew I wanted to do this, and they encouraged me to follow through, saying you would be reasonable."

When her stream of words finally stopped, Trevor turned

and faced her. "I'll think about it."

Shelly stared a moment as if she expected a discussion or an argument. "Thanks," she said finally and looked down at the table. Then she pushed away from it. "Excuse me, but I'm exhausted. I think I'd better turn in."

"Me too. I run early in the mornings. I'll get the dishes before I head out back," he said. "You go on."

The hallway was illuminated only by soft light glowing from the entrances to the living room and her bedroom. Shelly's attention was drawn to the living room where a lamp glowed on an end table beside a recliner. Her eyes lit upon the bookshelf built into the wall behind the chair. Reminding herself that if she were serious about getting to know Trevor, then it was time to begin, she walked to the shelves and reached for one of Trevor's books. After reading the flyleaf, she turned it over. On the back was a picture of Trevor—a handsome man.

She ran her fingers over the picture, the face so much like Don's, but with more maturity. Don had greatly admired his older brother.

Hearing a movement, she turned. Trevor stood not three feet away. She knew he must have seen her staring at his picture. "I thought I might read myself to sleep," she said, trying to redeem herself, but quickly realized, "That's not a compliment, is it?"

"The worst of insults to a writer," he said, but he grinned.

"Oh, does the radio on the nightstand have an alarm?"

"It does. What time do you want to get up?"

"In time to run with you. That is, if you don't mind."

"I'll set the clock."

He went to her room and picked up the clock-radio, feeling an incredible sense of optimism. Shelly had not run from him today.

She had asked, *Do you mind if I run with you?*
Mind?

Ah!

Mind, indeed.

Imagine. He and Shelly Landon running together!

thirteen

It was early afternoon that Tuesday before Shelly and Maria returned from their shopping spree, laughing and laden with packages. Trevor came out of his office after a productive day of writing spurred on by an unusual amount of inspiration.

Shelly was enthralled with the spirit of the island, the international blend of people, the smiling faces, and the contrast of mountains and beaches as they drove to and from the shopping center.

"I could spend a month at that shopping center and still not see it all. It was wonderful. The shaded sidewalks, the courtyards. Did you know they offer classes in hula? If I were going to be here long enough, I'd take that. And you can learn to make leis. Oh—and how to cut pineapple." She looked at Maria. "I would figure you'd do it like coconuts—crack them open with a hammer."

Shelly and Maria went shopping for groceries after lunch, then called Trevor from the guest house a short while before supper was ready.

After he was seated at the table, the two of them proudly brought in the dishes. "And there are few calories and very little fat," Shelly said, looking over the array of steamed summer vegetables, rice, coleslaw, and the specialty: grilled jumbo island prawns prepared in Trevor's favorite way, sautéed with tomato and oyster sauce.

While Maria busied herself in the kitchen, Trevor asked Shelly to elaborate on her plans for the future.

"A lot depends upon who owns the health club. If I can buy it, then the price will determine how much I have to work to make the loan payments, whether that is to you, the bank, my parents, or whomever."

"Then mightn't it be best if we keep the arrangement like it is? There are no payments to make, and you're free to do as you please with the club."

"Not really. I have to consider what you might think, and I'm always aware that the profits are yours so I can't take too many chances or consider investing."

"What would you like to do, Shelly, if money were no object?"

"I'm sure that will always be, regardless," she said, "but if it were mine, I would take a chance on hiring Jake full-time as evening manager. I would cut down on the classes I teach. You see, I've had opportunities to speak to groups since the publicity on an exercise night for the handicapped. But something I'd really like to do is be involved with those who have lost their loved ones. Those, like myself, who seem to have everything going for them, but still need help in facing loss and grief. I think it's especially hard for young people."

"Something like victim's assistance programs?" Trevor asked, interested.

"On a smaller scale than that. I think relatives and friends of victims of crime or terminal illness or accidents need professional help as well as what I'm thinking of. There are a number of programs already in existence for grieving loved ones, but I think the younger people need a support system targeted for them. Now that I've lost Don, gone through the scare of my dad's heart attack, and then faced Gran's death, I'm aware that these things can happen. But I'd never encounted that when Don died. It was a shock to discover that my life was not going to work out the way I had taken for granted."

"And you'll only do this if the health club is yours?"

She shook her head. "No. Now that the idea is part of me—more so as I'm talking about it—I know I'll do it. I picture it as a national organization with chapters, and I even think I'd

like to travel around and talk to those people, let them know I
. . .understand."

How easy, he thought, it would be to tell Shelly that of
course she can have the health club and that I will help her
fulfill her dreams if she wants. He could even return to North
Carolina and take over half the responsibility. But she would-
n't want that.

He could also tell her that he never took seriously her
remark about giving him her half of the club. Gran had left it
to her. It was hers. But the moment he would tell her she
could have the health club, which he fully intended to do, she
would sever all ties with him. She would never need him or
consult with him on anything. He wanted to keep her with
him a while longer. He'd made a success of pretending. He'd
pretend a while longer.

Through the rest of the evening, Trevor did just that. After
dinner he pretended he was simply a friend when she lounged
on the patio, reading his book, and he sat in a chair, editing
the hard copy of what he'd written earlier in the day. Then
later, he kept pretending they were just friends when she
asked if he wanted to work out with her in his gym, which of
course he did.

Then she decided to shower and turn in early. "I want to be
fresh in the morning," she said, "and be sure I'm warmed up
for Mike."

Trevor took his laptop down to the guest house and tried
to enter his corrections, knowing sleep would not come easily.
At one point, he walked down by the beach, looking up at
the brilliant stars, his thoughts floating heavenward. The more
he encouraged Shelly to explore her world, he realized, the
greater the likelihood that he would lose her forever.

❧

The following morning, after Shelly warmed up, Mike and
his crew arrived. Soon afterward, their cameras were set up
and the show started.

Mike introduced Shelly as a guest aerobics instructor from North Carolina and mentioned her credentials along with her having won the aerobics contest. Applause sounded from the onlookers, who by now included many Kalula residents who had gathered for the occasion.

"Now, let's get that body rolling," Mike encouraged. "Step. Step. Step. Step."

It reminded Trevor of the high school and college days when Shelly cheered, "Two, four, six, eight. Who do we appreciate? Don! Don! Don! Don!"

In the background was not a football team but high purple mountains and blue languid water. Now echoing in his mind was, "Step, step, step, step. Swing, swing, swing, swing. With Mike! Mike! Mike! Mike!"

"Take it Shelly," Mike said.

"One. Two. Three. Four."

"Come on now."

"Five. Six. Seven. Eight."

"One more set."

"One. Two. Three. Four."

"You can do it."

"Five. Six. Seven. Eight."

The marching of tennis shoes on rubber mats tapped in rhythmic unison.

During a break, much to the chagrin of Trevor, Mike told his viewing audience that the author Trevor Steinbord had invited them to Kalula for the filming of this program to be run on his TV program next week. The camera swung around toward Trevor, who smiled and nodded briefly. While this wasn't exactly his idea of a claim to fame, most of all Trevor didn't want Shelly to think he'd extended the invitation for any publicity purposes of his own.

☙

That evening, Shelly reclined in the lounge chair on the patio, beneath the shade of several palms that shielded her from the rays of the early evening sun. She looked beyond the pool, the garden, the palms, and even the expanse of ocean to where ocean met sky in an indistinct blur.

"Mind if I join you?" said Trevor, coming up beside her.

She looked up. "It's your home, Trevor," she said lightly, "I'm the guest, remember."

He laughed lightly and sat down in the chair where he'd sat the previous night, working on his papers while she read. He laid a file folder on the small table. "Yes," he said, "but you appeared deep in thought."

"Not. . .really deep," she said.

"Tired?" he asked.

"I'm drained," she admitted. "I feel like I've worked every bone, muscle, and sinew. But. . .it's an invigorating tiredness."

"For instance?" he prompted.

Taking a deep breath, she gazed toward the gently swaying palm fronds and the tiny peaks of white foam waltzing on the surface of the sea. As Shelly considered her reply, Maria came from house, rolling a cart laden with fresh fruit and coffee. Trevor and Shelly again expressed their gratitude for all the work Maria had done that day. Mike's crew had packed up their equipment and left at lunchtime, but Mike and the girls who exercised with him stayed for lunch and conversation on the patio and a mid-afternoon dip in the pool. Maria and her husband had cleaned up, then later she had presented Shelly and Trevor with a delightful dinner. Now, she brought them an evening snack.

"Oh, I was so glad to be part of it and to meet Mike and those pretty girls. I'm glad you enjoyed it. Will you want the same tomorrow?" Maria asked.

"Mike says we'll be finished by mid-morning, and he has to meet somebody for lunch," Shelly said.

While Maria and Trevor began discussing some household details, Shelly sat up. As she swung her legs over the side of the lounge chair, she noticed they had tanned from having exercised in the sun. She reached for the coffee pot and waved away Maria's gesture to pour. *I'm pouring Trevor Steinbord a cup of coffee! Will miracles never cease?*

After Maria left, Trevor handed Shelly several sheets of paper. "I've made a few suggestions concerning the project we discussed last evening."

She took the papers, excitement churning in her. "Then you think it's workable?"

"It's a great concept, Shelly. I can visualize it having far-reaching effects. There are programs for the close relatives who have lost loved ones, but nothing that I know of for those others who grieve. Yet their loss is real, too. But you need to be prepared for the results of such an undertaking. You need to be prepared for the demands the program will make on you as it grows, including traveling, speaking, and contending with publicity demands such as making appearances on talk shows."

With trepidation, Shelly looked at the typewritten pages. As she read, she became awed at the possibilities. Trevor had even suggested she gather the stories of grief-stricken friends and relatives and compile them into a book, which would reach more persons, more quickly, than the slower route of forming local chapters throughout the nation. That could be a beginning. From there, the possibilities would expand.

"This is. . .so much," Shelly said, feeling overwhelmed.

"You can start on a smaller scale, but I know you've always gone into things wholeheartedly."

"Where angels fear to tread," she admitted. "I was warned about starting a program for the handicapped and knew I couldn't handle that, so I've turned that over to professionals."

Shelly studied the papers and could see the possibilities. But she couldn't possibly undertake a project of such magnitude. "I hadn't really thought it through," she said, slightly downcast. "It's too big for me to handle, isn't it?"

"Definitely," he answered, and her face fell. Then he glanced toward the sky and back. Something glimmered in his eyes and a grin settled on his lips.

Shelly caught her breath as she met Trevor's gaze. She told herself that the unfamiliar pounding of her heart was because of all the work that stood before her. It couldn't possibly have anything to do with the warmth of Trevor's eyes when he looked at her.

Quickly averting her eyes, Shelly looked at the papers. "Let's. . .discuss it."

❧

On Thursday morning, the crew arrived again. Trevor didn't need to walk down to the beach. He knew what was happening. Mike and Shelly would be side by side on the black rubber discs, kicking their legs, bending their backs, swinging their arms, and loving every sweating minute of it. Three beautiful-bodied girls in tights would be doing the same thing behind them.

After the morning's taping, Shelly rushed in. "Guess what?" Her shining eyes and exuberance reminded Trevor of years past when she had information to impart to his family. At last, she was addressing him. Unfortunately, her excitement was brought on by another man.

"Mike wants me to make a video with him. He's going out of town for a week, but as soon as he gets back we can start," she announced. "This is great, Trevor. Do you realize what this can do for my. . .our. . .the health club?"

He could. And being imaginative as he was, he could even picture a chain of health clubs, all the way from North Carolina to Hawaii, with the appealing alliterative name of Landon/Lacuna Lifestyles.

Soon, Mike and his girls appeared. Mike again thanked Trevor for his hospitality and suggested they all go out and celebrate that evening. He thanked them but declined. If Mike

Lacuna was the man Shelly wanted and needed, then he would be glad for her. But he didn't have to watch their relationship develop.

❧

Late that evening, after having coffee alone, Trevor worked for hours at his computer until finally he heard a car drive up. Several minutes later Shelly walked onto the deck and peeked into his lighted office. Trevor lifted his hand in acknowledgment, then closed his file, turned off the computer, and joined her on the deck.

"How was your evening?" he asked, seating himself in a chair near her.

"Fun," she said. "Several more of Mike's friends joined us. We went to the—now I've forgotten, after saying it over and over, and it was the last thing I asked Mike before I got out of his car. Anyway, it was a Japanese restaurant. . .something Zen."

"Restaurant Izakaya Zen," Trevor said.

"That's it!" She lifted her hand and pushed her hair behind her shoulder. "You should have gone with us. Most of the evening was spent talking about you."

"Me?" he said, surprised.

She nodded. "They wanted to discuss your books and all about your life in North Carolina. They told me things that I knew nothing about. That you speak out on injustices in your frequent interviews, are involved in projects to help the needy, donate to charities. . ."

Fearing Trevor might be embarrassed, Shelly quickly added, "You know, Mike thinks our making the tape will help both our careers."

Trevor turned and stepped over to the wooden railing, looking out into the night.

Shelly felt a sudden cool breeze. "But not here," she added quickly. "We won't take up any more of your time."

Trevor closed his eyes momentarily as his heart tightened

in his chest. What he had feared was coming to pass before his eyes—and he had promoted it. Shelly was falling for another man.

fourteen

"Spectacular," Shelly said as she and Trevor arrived at the beach where the luau was held. The sunset looked as if a fairy godmother had swung her wand and sprinkled the sea with gold, changed the beach to pumpkin orange, and painted the sky a robin's throat red.

It matched Shelly's festive mood and the bright hand-painted silk Hawaiian dress she wore which fit her figure like a soft glove. Trevor, in slacks and short-sleeved aloha shirt, became part of the magic as he led her to the tables on the beach, bordered on one side by palms, where they watched the yellow sun slide into the golden ocean.

Trevor sipped a fruit drink which Shelly thought looked especially appealing, garnished with mint and a pineapple wedge speared with a maraschino cherry on a toothpick. As the light of day ended, a torchlighting ceremony began with a conch shell being blown to produce its haunting signal.

Then a royal court appeared. "Dressed like their ancestors of one hundred years ago," Trevor said, as the young people in costume circled a pit and began chanting.

"What are they doing?" Shelly whispered, leaning toward Trevor.

He bent toward her, his whispered words tickling her ear. "There's a pig in there, covered with ti leaves. It's been roasting all day. The pit is called an imu. Now, they're praying."

The young people gracefully lifted their hands and gazed toward heaven, offering thanks.

"They're chanting in native Hawaiian," Trevor said.

Shelly's gaze followed theirs and she saw that the moon had risen high and bright. Looking at Trevor, she saw that the winking of the stars reflected in his eyes. "The luau has begun," he said emphatically.

Then came the variety of foods from which to choose. "Lomi-lomi salmon," Trevor explained. "Lomilomi is a form of massage they apply to the salmon which releases its natural flavor."

"Interesting," Shelly said. "But I want the pig."

"One kalua pig coming up."

She poked him playfully with an elbow. "Leave some for the others."

He laughed. "You must try the mahimahi."

"What is it?"

He shook his head. "Try it first." He stabbed a piece with his fork and she accepted it, chewed, began to nod, "Mmmm. Great!"

"Porpoise." he said.

She felt momentarily stunned, then reached for her glass and held it suspended, as if in a toast, while she swallowed hard.

"Celebrating?" he asked, with a grin.

"Well, my first time for. . .porpoise."

After fresh coconut cake for dessert, the notes of a conch shell marked the beginning of spectacular entertainment from the South Pacific. Hula dancers swayed gracefully and spoke with their hands accompanied by the songs of Old Hawaii, Tahiti, Fiji, Samoa, and New Zealand.

When the songs finished, the hula dancers went into the audience to choose people to go on stage and learn the hula.

"They'll choose you," Trevor said.

"No they won't," she protested.

He gazed deeply into her eyes and said, "Yes they will—because you're so beautiful."

Too surprised to demur when a dancer approached her, she soon joined other selected members of the audience in attempting the rhythmic flow of the traditional dance. Each student had to perform a solo number while the audience laughed and applauded, with Trevor being the most enthusiastic during her performance.

"How was I?" she asked as she leaned back against her chair where his arm happened to be.

"Exotic," he said emphatically, his face close to hers. The audience began to applaud. Shelly looked toward the stage as dancers began their spectacular fire-knife extravaganza.

Looking again at Trevor, Shelly saw that reflected flames sparked his eyes. His hand grasped her shoulder. Were she not so overwhelmed, she might have said, "I agree," when he whispered close to her ear, "This is special."

❧

The magic continued long after the music stopped. Trevor led Shelly along Waikiki beach to where the silver-tipped sea caressed the shore and gently nudged the star-studded sky. Maybe it was the atmosphere that changed them, maybe it was the feeling of having been in another world, another era, during the luau.

"I loved it," she said softly, and the words floated on the breeze. Trevor turned toward her. He could not, as he had thought, be content with whatever crumbs of her time she would allow. He should not have turned, should not have grasped her shoulders as the gentle breeze lifted her hair away.

He felt the brush of her hair against his arms and the feel of soft silk beneath his fingers. Her head tilted back, and her face, bathed in moonlight, lifted to his as he drew her closer and bent his head. The intoxicating scent of her filled his senses.

Run from me Shelly, as you've always done, part of him was saying, while another part was pleading that she say, not "I loved it," but rather, "I love you."

He ignored her questioning eyes, her incomprehension. As if drawn by a magnet, his lips covered hers. He felt as if he were in over his head, felt the power of the undertow that required all his strength to fight, lest he drown. He forced his way into calmer waters, mentally stepped onto the shore before the tide carried him into danger. "Shelly," he whispered roughly, and a lifetime of longing was in his voice.

❧

Hearing him whisper her name in such ragged tones made Shelly want to be closer, and as he attempted to move away, she drew his face down to hers again. It was as if he had reached into her soul, bringing out all the stored-up desires that she thought she could never express. Her hungry heart, starved for so long, was feeding on the warmth and wonder of him. And for the moment nothing seemed important but the feel of his lips on hers, awakening in her the need to love and be loved.

She felt him withdraw, resist her, and she reluctantly loosened her hands from around his neck, lowered her head, and stepped back as he moved his hands down her arms and caught hers in his own, holding them tightly.

Shelly felt the flood descending from her eyes and turned from him, ashamed that she could have so abandoned herself to him emotionally, embarrassed that he was the one to pull away.

"I'm sorry," she choked out.

"I didn't mean to make you cry," he said gently.

She shook her head, still unable to look at him. "It's not you. It's. . .me."

With their backs to the magic of the evening, the drive home was like facing reality. He drove in silence, with that distant, unreadable expression on his face. She knew he would think she had cried because she was upset with him, but how could she explain her response to him? Or. . .to herself?

Shelly spent the night in a dreamworld where she was enveloped in strong, loving, protective arms. She never wanted them to let her go.

❧

In the light of a new day, Shelly told herself she'd feel differently after a rejuvenating shower. She stepped into the tub and lifted her face to the streaming, steaming liquid. But after she turned off the water and dried herself she admitted the feel of Trevor's touch had not been washed away—had not disappeared down the drain. He had awakened in her a response to him that she suspected would never sleep again.

After making herself presentable in shorts and T-shirt and towel-drying her hair into damp curls, she went into the kitchen and saw that he'd shaved, dressed casually, and already made breakfast.

Shelly traced the rim of her orange juice glass, then sighed and clasped her fingers on her lap. "I feel I need to explain last night. My. . .response, I mean."

"There's nothing to explain," he said gently.

Her eyes flashed. "I don't go around throwing myself at men. Other than a friendly peck, I haven't kissed anyone since Don. It's been such a long time and I. . .didn't think I could."

Trevor quickly got up to refill his coffee cup. He stood with his back to Shelly, looking out the window.

"But then, I guess you're used to women coming on to you," she accused, when he returned to the table.

"I've been friends with many women, but I've never given away my heart, never my complete devotion. I've made it clear from the onset of any friendship that it couldn't lead to a lifetime commitment."

"Because your writing is first in your life?

"My writing is second," he corrected. "Apparently, I can't have what is first."

Thinking he probably wouldn't answer, she asked anyway. "Which book is that in?"

"All of them," he said seriously, "but most obviously in the first one. I was too much an amateur to be able to hide it behind fictional characters. Now stop worrying about last night. Remember, I've known you all your life, and I'm not about to make any snap judgments about your character."

Shelly relaxed slightly, but she couldn't figure out why Trevor's eyes held such a mixture of hope and sadness.

❧

During the entire week that followed, Shelly felt the magic of the luau night had returned. She and Trevor ran in the early morning, then he worked in his office for a few hours while she either worked on plans for the health club, read, or talked with Maria. Then in the afternoons and evenings Trevor held her hand when he took her island-hopping, lay his arm around her shoulders when pointing out pineapple fields and volcanoes, performed shenanigans under water that almost made her lose her snorkel, brushed his lips lightly across hers during a moon-lit cruise.

On Sunday morning they attended a worship service on the beach, then that evening they had coffee on the patio and watched the sun set.

Shelly inhaled deeply of the fragrant air. "This has been the most wonderful vacation of my life. I'm going to hate to leave here." She could hardly believe the change in herself since she'd come to Hawaii. It seemed like a different life-time when she had harbored those childish resentments against Trevor.

He'd done so much for her—taught her to reach out to other people—and now she feared she'd perhaps reached too far toward Trevor. His own words warned her not to come too close. First he'd pulled away from her that night on the beach, and then he'd made it clear the next morning that he'd loved and lost—and because of that love he couldn't give his heart to any woman.

Then why should she stay in Hawaii any longer—only to be torn apart by her mixed up feelings—only to chance a deeper heartbreak? No. . .since she was tempted to stay, she felt it wise that she leave.

Just then the phone rang. It was Mike Lacuna, and Trevor handed Shelly the cordless phone as he went inside the house. Once she got off the phone, Shelly explained that Mike would come for her early thé next morning to start taping their video.

He did. . .and she didn't return until late that night.

"The taping went like clockwork," Shelly told Trevor excitedly. "Like the two of us had been exercising together all our lives."

Then she called the airport to confirm a departure time for leaving Hawaii.

ta

The next day, Trevor loaded her bags in the trunk of his car. When he came back into the house, she was sliding his book back into its slot on the bookshelf.

"Did you finish it?" he asked.

She shook her head. She really wasn't too keen on reading about the love of his life. "There wasn't time."

"Take it with you," he said, so she dropped it in her totebag.

Strange, after all the things they'd accomplished together, the relationship they'd built, the fun they'd had, the careers they'd discussed, there seemed to be little to talk about on the way to the airport. Not being prone to silence, Shelly began to talk about the club. "You know, Trevor, those exercise tapes will really boost our business. And Mike said he'd love to come by and make personal appearances—autograph his pictures or something."

Without responding, Trevor kept looking out at the road where there really wasn't all that much traffic.

Shelly shook her head. Surely he didn't think she should ask for his autograph on his book! No, she'd feel silly doing that. It wasn't like she was a fan or anything. An uneasiness settled upon her, as if she were reverting to that uncomfortable feeling she used to have whenever she was with Trevor.

When it was time to board the plane, Trevor handed her an

envelope. "In here is a copy of the initial arrangements about the health club. I could have given it to you sooner, but I didn't want you thinking I had some ulterior motive. It's yours, free and clear."

"What?" she said, disbelieving. "Why would you. . . ?"

"If you want to know why I did what I'm doing," he said, taking his book from her totebag, "you'll find the answer in here."

He turned to the first page and pointed to the words, *Dedicated to my heroine.*

"That's you, Shelly. I'm not the hero in the book, just the main character."

Shelly felt a sense of panic as she tried to figure out how on earth to respond to his words. Uncertain emotions tumbled through her.

Trevor shook his head, placed his finger on her lips, then kissed her. "Be happy, Shelly Landon. I wish you every success. I want what is best for you. I always have."

He watched her walk away. At the last moment she turned, still wearing her shocked expression, and lifted her hand in a parting gesture.

Trevor returned to his house, went straight to his office, and began to write as if his life depended upon it. Which it did. Fortunately, he wrote equally well, whether from inspiration or desperation. His characters, at least, had the good sense to retain a semblance of dignity rather than bare their souls in foolish endeavors doomed to failure.

fifteen

At first, Shelly didn't believe it.

Then, as she continued to read, she began to see herself through the main character's eyes—not as a spoiled brat, not as a silly girl with only cheerleading on her mind, not as a nuisance invading his family's home and wreaking havoc. In the character's eyes she was a person of both external and internal beauty, excitement, and potential, and she had wiggled her way into his heart in spite of all his attempts to rationalize her age, his age, and her complete devotion to his younger brother.

Would I have suspected the heroine is based on me if he hadn't said so? Shelly wondered. Maybe, she decided, she would have suspected it was based on his life in North Carolina, although his setting was elsewhere. But she would not have suspected it was she that he loved. That realization would not have come easily.

Even now, it didn't.

But the more she read, the more engrossed and astounded she became. Here she was, thirty thousand feet above the ocean, learning that Trevor Steinbord had loved her.

She was in a race, trying to finish the book before the plane landed in Los Angeles. Some of it she could skim. For once, she was grateful she had a layover, and after landing, she continued reading until she finished. After closing the book she stared at Trevor's picture on the back cover. He was younger then, about the same age as she had been when she lost Don.

How incredible! He'd spent many years learning what he'd taught her—to reach out to other people and to retain the memory of love but not let it destroy. He'd apparently worked hard at getting over her—and he'd succeeded. But why hadn't he told her in person? Was he afraid she'd lash out at him as she had done for so many years? Or was he acting like the self-sacrificing hero in his movie?

Maybe if she read his other books, she'd have some clue. She went to the gift shops in the airport, but they didn't carry his books. Deciding to have an orange juice, she went to a snack shop. Suddenly she remembered the official-looking envelope Trevor had handed her.

It appeared legal, all right, and seemed to turn complete ownership over to her. But something was strange. While there were lines for both their signatures, it wasn't signed. That would have to be done before she could move forward with her plans.

She downed the juice, found a phone, and dialed his number. After the third ring, the answering machine came on. "Trevor," she began. "You didn't sign the papers for the health club. Do I need to mail them back, or can you get another copy, or what?" She paused, uncomfortable with talking to a machine. She needed to say *something,* though.

"I finished the book, and," she cleared her throat, "I'm surprised, to say the least. But it's so noisy in here I can't hear myself think. Anyway, I understand why it ended, not happily, but honorably." Then on impulse, she added. "But about the movie made of your other book. Since your main characters were all adults, I still think your professor was a coward."

Feeling foolish for not knowing what else to say, or how to say it, she simply said "Well, hope to hear from you soon. Good-bye."

After boarding the plane, headed home to North Carolina, Shelly stared out the window at the darkness.

Regardless of where her thoughts wandered, they always returned to the subject of Trevor Steinbord. There were still so many unanswered questions. Why had he wanted her in Hawaii? Why had he tried so hard to make her like him? Why had he made her love him?

He made me. . .what?

Love him?

Love him!

Shelly let out a gasp of surprise, then quickly covered her mouth, fearing she might wake the entire plane. *I love Trevor Steinbord!*

In one sense it was a tremendous surprise, but in another it seemed perfectly natural.

But am I going to let him know such a thing? So he can tell me to get over it? So he can punish me the way I've punished him for so long?

Why must loving be so painful?

❧

After arriving home, Shelly hedged and told the families they'd get together soon and she would tell them all about her trip. She just couldn't face them yet, not after having discovered what they all probably knew, and not without having Trevor's signature on the legal papers. She kept calling and kept getting the answering machine saying he was out of town.

"Go on home, Jake," she said the second night after she arrived back in North Carolina. "I want to go over some paper work." Jake turned out all the lights except in her office and left.

As Shelly poured over the papers, she heard a noise and quickly rose from her chair to look out into the darkened club.

He walked toward the light streaming from her doorway. She let out a gasp of surprise and backed away from the grim expression on his face and the threat in his eyes. "What are you doing here?"

"A coward?" he boomed, ignoring that question.

"Well. . ." she began.

Then he held out the key he'd used to get in the door. "I forgot to give you this."

"I tried to call you, but I kept getting your answering machine."

"That's because I was on my way to see you. To tell you, Shelly, that I love you."

Her heart was racing and she backed up to the other side of her desk.

Relentlessly, he pursued her. "Now are those the words of a coward?" His hands were on her arms and his face very close to hers.

She began in a small voice, "You're making progress, but I'm not totally convinced."

His eyes held hers, and she knew it was no longer a game. "Will you give me a lifetime to prove it, Shelly? Can you love me?"

Can I? Her heart was in her eyes. "I do love you, Trevor." The wonder of it for them both was overwhelming.

Shelly was never sure quite how it happened, but the next thing she knew, she was in Trevor Steinbord's arms, being thoroughly kissed.

Moments later, Shelly admitted, "I might not be the easiest person in the world to live with."

"It may be difficult," he laughed, "but with the help of God, all things are possible."

"You're lucky you smiled when you said that!"

A Letter To Our Readers

Dear Reader:

In order that we might better contribute to your reading enjoyment, we would appreciate your taking a few minutes to respond to the following questions. When completed, please return to the following:

Rebecca Germany, Managing Editor
Heartsong Presents
P.O. Box 719
Uhrichsville, Ohio 44683

1. Did you enjoy reading *Hawaiian Heartbeat?*
   - ❑ Very much. I would like to see more books by this author!
   - ❑ Moderately
     I would have enjoyed it more if _____

     _____

2. Are you a member of **Heartsong Presents**? ❑ Yes ❑ No
   If no, where did you purchase this book? _____

   _____

3. What influenced your decision to purchase this book? (Check those that apply.)

❑ Cover	❑ Back cover copy
❑ Title	❑ Friends
❑ Publicity	❑ Other_____

4. How would you rate, on a scale from 1 (poor) to 5 (superior), the cover design? _____

5. On a scale from 1 (poor) to 10 (superior), please rate the following elements.

    ___Heroine   ___Plot

    ___Hero   ___Inspirational theme

    ___Setting   ___Secondary characters

6. What settings would you like to see covered in **Heartsong Presents** books?_____

_____

_____

7. What are some inspirational themes you would like to see treated in future books?_____

_____

_____

8. Would you be interested in reading other **Heartsong Presents** titles?   ❏ Yes   ❏ No

9. Please check your age range:
    ❏ Under 18   ❏ 18-24   ❏ 25-34
    ❏ 35-45   ❏ 46-55   ❏ Over 55

10. How many hours per week do you read? _____

Name _____

Occupation _____

Address _____

City_____ State_____ Zip _____

Heart♥ng

CONTEMPORARY ROMANCE IS CHEAPER BY THE DOZEN!

Any 12 Heartsong Presents titles for only $26.95 **

Buy any assortment of twelve Heartsong Presents titles and save 25% off of the already discounted price of $2.95 each!

**plus $1.00 shipping and handling per order and sales tax where applicable.

HEARTSONG PRESENTS *TITLES AVAILABLE NOW:*

__HP 38 A PLACE TO CALL HOME, *Eileen M. Berger*

__HP 41 FIELDS OF SWEET CONTENT, *Norma Jean Lutz*

__HP 49 YESTERDAY'S TOMORROWS, *Linda Herring*

__HP 54 HOME TO HER HEART, *Lena Nelson Dooley*

__HP 57 LOVE'S SILKEN MELODY, *Norma Jean Lutz*

__HP 58 FREE TO LOVE, *Doris English*

__HP 61 PICTURE PERFECT, *Susan Kirby*

__HP 62 A REAL AND PRECIOUS THING, *Brenda Bancroft*

__HP 66 AUTUMN LOVE, *Ann Bell*

__HP 69 BETWEEN LOVE AND LOYALTY, *Susannah Hayden*

__HP 70 A NEW SONG, *Kathleen Yapp*

__HP 73 MIDSUMMER'S DREAM, *Rena Eastman*

__HP 81 BETTER THAN FRIENDS, *Sally Laity*

__HP 82 SOUTHERN GENTLEMEN, *Yvonne Lehman*

__HP 85 LAMP IN DARKNESS, *Connie Loraine*

__HP 86 POCKETFUL OF LOVE, *Loree Lough*

__HP 89 CONTAGIOUS LOVE, *Ann Bell*

__HP 90 CATER TO A WHIM, *Norma Jean Lutz*

__HP 94 TO BE STRONG, *Carolyn R. Scheidies*

__HP102 IF GIVEN A CHOICE, *Tracie J. Peterson*

__HP106 RAGDOLL, *Kelly R. Stevens*

__HP109 INSPIRED LOVE, *Ann Bell*

__HP110 CALLIE'S MOUNTAIN, *Veda Boyd Jones*

__HP113 BETWEEN THE MEMORY AND THE MOMENT, *Susannah Hayden*

__HP114 THE QUIET HEART, *Rae Simons*

__HP117 FARTHER ALONG THE ROAD, *Susannah Hayden*

__HP118 FLICKERING FLAMES, *Connie Loraine*

__HP121 THE WINNING HEART, *Norma Jean Lutz*

__HP122 THERE'S ALWAYS TOMORROW, *Brenda Bancroft*

__HP125 LOVE'S TENDER GIFT, *Elizabeth Murphy*

__HP126 MOUNTAIN MAN, *Yvonne Lehman*

__HP129 SEARCH FOR YESTERDAY, *Mary Hawkins*

__HP130 A MATTER OF SECURITY, *Kay Cornelius*

__HP133 A CHANGE OF HEART, *Nancy Lavo*

__HP134 THE ROAD HOME, *Susannah Hayden*

__HP137 DISTANT LOVE, *Ann Bell*

__HP138 ABIDING LOVE, *Elizabeth Murphy*

__HP142 FLYING HIGH, *Phyllis A. Humphrey*

__HP146 DANCING IN THE DARKNESS, *Janelle Burnham*

__HP149 LLAMA LAND, *VeraLee Wiggins*

(If ordering from this page, please remember to include it with the order form.)

Presents

Heart♥ng Presents
Love Stories Are Rated G!

That's for godly, gratifying, and of course, great! If you love a thrilling love story, but don't appreciate the sordidness of some popular paperback romances, **Heartsong Presents** is for you. In fact, **Heartsong Presents** is the *only inspirational romance book club*, the only one featuring love stories where Christian faith is the primary ingredient in a marriage relationship.

Sign up today to receive your first set of four, never before published Christian romances. Send no money now; you will receive a bill with the first shipment. You may cancel at any time without obligation, and if you aren't completely satisfied with any selection, you may return the books for an immediate refund!

Imagine. . .four new romances every four weeks—two historical, two contemporary—with men and women like you who long to meet the one God has chosen as the love of their lives. . .all for the low price of $9.97 postpaid.

To join, simply complete the coupon below and mail to the address provided. **Heartsong Presents** romances are rated G for another reason: They'll arrive *Godspeed!*

YES! Sign me up for Heart♥ng!

NEW MEMBERSHIPS WILL BE SHIPPED IMMEDIATELY!
Send no money now. We'll bill you only $9.97 post-paid with your first shipment of four books. Or for faster action, call toll free 1-800-847-8270.

NAME _____

ADDRESS _____

CITY _____ STATE _____ ZIP _____

MAIL TO: HEARTSONG PRESENTS, P.O. Box 719, Uhrichsville, Ohio 44683

YES10-96